AN IRISH HEARTBEAT

by

Paul Ferris

Grosvenor House
Publishing Limited

Paul Ferris is hereby identified as author of this
work in accordance with Section 77 of the Copyright, Designs
and Patents Act 1988

The book cover picture is copyright to Bernie Rosage Jr

This book is published by
Grosvenor House Publishing Ltd
28-30 High Street, Guildford, Surrey, GU1 3HY.
www.grosvenorhousepublishing.co.uk

A CIP record for this book
is available from the British Library

ISBN 978-1-907652-26-4

For Geraldine

'....*My childhood days bring back sad reflections*
Of happy times I spent so long ago
My boyhood friends and my own relations
Have all passed on now like melting snow....'

(Carrickfergus)

Biography

Paul Ferris was born in 1965. He left his native Northern Ireland in 1981 to pursue a career as a Professional Footballer. He lives in Northumberland with his wife and three children.

1

He awoke on a bed he'd last slept in 22 years ago. As the morning sun stabbed its way through the defenceless curtains, the strange familiarity of the room unnerved him. Many times he had told himself he would never return. For too long, he had been afraid to come back. As he cast his eyes around the cramped and dusty room, he felt as though he had stepped into another lifetime.

Every part of the bedroom was as he remembered it. Yet everything was different. It was as if the entire colour had been sucked out of it over the years. It was a room no longer of its time. He lay in the silence and ran his hand along the faded blue wall he once helped his father to paint. He thought of the last time he lay in this bed. She was by his side then. He hoped she would be there forever, until he destroyed himself and abandoned her. No, it wasn't his old bedroom that had changed, it was him. This was the room of his innocence. Today, he was looking at it through a distorted lens. He'd changed so much since he last called this place his home.

He reviewed the events of the last two days. The dreaded phone call from Tom, when he knew by the tone of his brother's voice, the rest of the conversation would not be a good one. There were the deliberations about whether to return at all, and then the argument with Maggie on his arrival. What was the argument about?

What was it Maggie said that irritated him so much? Why did even being in the same room as her make him feel so uncomfortable? He intended staying at Maggie's, but left in a rush, and instead he and Annie had made their way here late last night. They moved between the tiny kitchen and the bedrooms. While he slept in his old room, Annie slept in his mother's bed. Downstairs in the living room, his mother Mary lay dead in an open casket.

Cormac was 40 years old yesterday. He was born and grew up in the village of Killane, on the edge of Belfast, at the height of Northern Ireland's bloody divisive conflict. He was raised by Catholic parents and educated by a combination of vicious priests and violent nuns. He was the youngest of three brothers and one sister.

His memories of childhood, although fading fast, were that he was essentially happy and loved. His brothers, Daniel and Tom, who were both much older than Cormac, loved him in a protective Irish way, because he was their 'baby' brother. Tom, the eldest, who'd never married, now ran a successful music store in West Belfast. He was one of the few people Cormac had kept in touch with over the last two decades. Daniel, a year younger than Tom, was the black sheep of the family until he died, aged 26, when Cormac was 10. He moved out of the family home at 17 but remained a regular visitor until his death. At the height of the 'troubles', he wandered drunkenly into the wrong place at the wrong time and was beaten to death with baseball bats and golf clubs in an alley in the warren of terraced houses that merged to form Belfast's 'peace line.' Maggie was different. She was born 13 years before him, on the same day, and he sometimes felt that their birthday was all they had in common. His earliest memories were of his fear of being left alone with her when his parents would go on their weekly visit to the local pub. No matter how hard he tried to 'be good,' Maggie always found some reason to punish him. After years of trying to impress her, to gain some respect from her, to connect with her, it no longer mattered to him what she thought, said or did.

'Dad, Dad, get up, Aunty Maggie and Uncle Jack will be here in a minute and we left the kitchen in a mess last night!'

Cormac looked up from the bed, and there before him stood his reason for living. With her red hair tumbling down her shoulders, bright blue eyes and a complexion as pale as snow, stood his one and only Annie. She never knew her mother. His wife Jill had died from the complications of Annie's birth. From that moment, he devoted his life equally to Annie and his career.

Cormac shook himself from the bed and stumbled to the bathroom. He splashed the icy water against his face.

'Christ, you look your age!'

He glanced in the bathroom mirror to see a smiling Annie hovering at the door. He stared at his reflection in the dimly lit mirror. His blue eyes, once his most attractive feature, were now sunken shells permanently framed by the black circles that appeared overnight in his late thirties. He was never sure whether this was the result of too much time spent in dingy rooms poring over ancient texts, or even more time spent in dingier pubs slumped over freshly poured drinks. He slapped some life into his pale and sagging cheeks.

'You can say that that again.'

He reached for his beautiful girl. He pulled her tightly to him and wished he could fast forward today's events. It took him by surprise when he felt the water trickle down his cheek and fall gently onto her hair.

'What time's Nan's funeral, dad?'

'11:30, I think.'

'Oh shit, that's in half an hour!'

He shook his head.

'Annie.'

'What?'

'You've got a filthy mouth!'

'Sorry, dad.'

'Annie.'

'What?'

'Guess what?'

'I know. You love me!'

After she'd had gone downstairs, Cormac walked wearily back to the bedroom. He opened the faded curtains. As the mid-morning sun illuminated the dull little bedroom, Cormac felt a shudder that began at his shoulders and made it all the way to his toes. On the wall to his right was every proud memento of his academic and sporting achievements. On the thin shelf that divided the wall in two, stood eight or nine dusty trophies, untouched since the day he left; an homage to a lost child. He studied the tired little space. This room, once the centre of his universe, felt like it belonged to someone else. So much had changed since he'd last slept here. His beloved father had long since passed on, and now his mother lay downstairs as silent as stone.

Annie snapped him from his melancholy.

'Dad, you've really got to come downstairs, the house is a mess and Aunty Maggie will be here any minute.

Besides, I found some eggs in the fridge and made some scrambled eggs.'

'I didn't know you could make scrambled eggs.'

'I can't. It started out as an omelette and just sort of became scrambled eggs!'

Cormac smiled and started towards the stairs.

'How long is it since we've been in Ireland, Annie?'

'Dad, I've never been in Ireland.'

He felt a surge of guilt. He had not set foot in Ireland since the day he scurried away as a terrified boy on a cold March night in 1987. How his life had changed. Today he sat in his childhood home as Cormac O'Reilly MP, junior minister at the Home Office. A former high-flying barrister, earmarked as a future prime minister. He'd achieved so much. Had he lost too much?

He pulled his chair up to the familiar kitchen table. He remembered the day his father had proudly brought it home, oblivious to the fact its presence in the narrow kitchen meant the back door would never fully open again. At this table he learned the art of eating with his elbows strapped tightly to his body, the only way he could get the food from the plate to his mouth without starting a war with Tom or Daniel. A war that, as the youngest, he knew he was certain to lose. He picked up his fork and scooped the egg to his mouth, elbow free and fully functioning.

'Annie, these eggs are fantastic. When you go off to university, promise me you'll look after yourself. I mean eat properly and try to cook fresh food,'

Annie pulled her chair next to his, reducing the effectiveness of his elbow in the process. She rested her head against his shoulder.

'You're definitely turning into the old fart you told me you would never be. Anyway, it's still three months until I go to Edinburgh, so can we just live in the moment a little?'

Her absentmindedness brought a smile to his face. This was certainly not a moment in his life he wanted to savour.

Annie leaned away from him.

'What's so funny, dad?'

'Well, much as I really enjoy your little moments of new-age spirituality and all that, I'm not exactly sure that this is a great time for living in the moment!'

The doorbell rang.

Annie got up and moved towards the door. Cormac was grateful for the space she created. He was also glad for the extra moment of peace before Maggie's arrival. He turned to his eggs. Annie turned back from the door.

'Dad, will you get it?'

Cormac pushed his eggs away.

'I'm not getting it. You get it!'

'She's your sister.'

He stood and moved toward the back of the kitchen, the furthest point in the house from where Maggie was now irritatingly holding her finger on the door bell.

'Annie, I know she is, but unfortunately she doesn't like me very much, and also scares the shit out of me!'

Annie sat herself down in front of his half-eaten breakfast.

'Dad, please just get the door … oh and by the way, you've got a filthy mouth!'

He could tell by her tone he was defeated and made his way down the narrow hall. He opened the door. Maggie's finger remained on the bell for longer than was necessary. She stepped into the cramped hallway and hugged him in the awkward way she had always done. Why was it no matter which way he tilted his head in preparation, she always managed to turn the same way? Did she do it deliberately? Cormac was angry with himself for the thought. Maggie marched past him.

'Where is she?'

'She's in the kitchen.'

Maggie spun towards him.

'Mammy's body's in the kitchen?'

Cormac, stifled an inappropriate laugh at the thought of his mother's body competing with the kitchen table.

'Sorry, Maggie, I thought you meant Annie. Mum is in the living room.'

Maggie turned on her heels and pushed open the living room door, just enough so that Cormac could glimpse the bottom of the casket. She fell to her knees. He turned his head away. Maggie wailed as he closed the door.

—◊—

2

Maggie eventually joined them in the cramped kitchen. Annie made coffee. Maggie didn't drink it. Maggie made tea.

'Doesn't she look peaceful, Cormac?'

Cormac didn't answer. He tried to count to ten.

'Cormac, I was just saying, doesn't Mammy look peaceful?'

Maggie was standing over him.

He told himself he didn't need to answer. He couldn't help himself.

'I wouldn't know, Maggie. Does she look peaceful?'

'What's that supposed to mean?'

'It means I don't wish to see my mum as a corpse. I don't wish to have a lasting memory of that, thanks!'

'But that was Mammy's wish, to have an open coffin, to have a Catholic burial, to have family around her.'

'Maggie, please let's not argue – not now, of all times. Just respect the fact I don't wish to take part in that part, OK?'

'Frankly, Cormac, it's not OK! It's not OK that you haven't been home to see her for 22 years. It's not OK she broke her heart every day for you. It's not OK you've forgotten who you are. It's not OK you've lost your soul. And it's not OK to call her Mum. She always has been and always will be Mammy, OK?'

He rose to face her.

'Listen you stupid....'

'Cormac! Maggie! For Christ's sake, stop it!'

Cormac turned to see his older brother Tom standing in the hall. He felt his eyes sting. He felt like a little boy again. He took comfort in his brother's arms.

'Now then, hotshot, how does it feel to be the talk of the town?'

Tom and Cormac sat at the kitchen table while Annie and Maggie produced endless cups of tea and sandwiches for a multitude of strangers who now seemed to have taken control of the house.

'Hopefully I'm not.'

'You're far too modest, brother. Your arrival has been the talk of this shit-hole since Mum died.'

'Don't you mean Mammy, Tom?'

'Don't tell me Maggie is already giving you a hard time for selling out to your English ways. Ignore her, she's grieving.'

'She just winds me up, Tom.'

'Listen, Cormac, there are things you don't know about, things that happened a long time ago and Maggie hasn't had it easy, just trust me on that and cut her a bit of slack.'

'What things?'

Tom sighed and patted his shoulder.

'I'm afraid today, my brother, isn't the time for such talk, and we must instead bury our mother.'

Maggie arrived in a flurry of plates.

'Father Mackie is here to say the rosary. Are you two coming into the living room?'

Cormac, who even as a child never understood the Catholic faith, with all of its rules and chanting, was about to have his second fight of the day with Maggie, when his big brother came to the rescue again.

'Maggie, love, you go on in and me and Cormac will kneel in the hall.'

He mumbled his way through the prayers he hadn't said for two decades and was astonished that he remembered every word, every pause, and every part of the ritual. He thought back to his childhood, to the many times his father made them kneel in the living room after dinner while they recited the rosary. He contemplated the endless nights he lay in bed and would be sprinkled with holy water when his father thought he was asleep. He cringed at the embarrassment of confession. Of turning from boy to man and telling the red-faced priest every detail. He thought of his mother, fiercely proud of her family and devoted to her Catholic God. The God he wished also to be devoted to. The God he prayed to every night in the small bedroom upstairs. The God that no matter how hard he tried, he'd never really believed in.

When the rosary had finished, he shook hands with familiar strangers and wondered how so many people could fit into such a small space as his mother's living room. Why did they want to? Maggie came to find him hiding in the sanctuary of the kitchen, which the strangers thankfully seemed to think was out of bounds for them.

'They're putting the lid on now. Are you sure you don't want to see her?'

He meant to tell her to go away. He intended to tell her to leave him alone, and to let him grieve in his own way. Instead he took her hand and walked into the living room. He wished he hadn't.

The funeral service passed in a blur; all incense and ritual. There was nothing personal about her life; just empty promises of a better place. He took no comfort from it. He knew he should never have gone into the room with Maggie. He should never have given in to her. All through the service, he frantically searched for images of his mother as a walking, talking, living person. He tried to conjure the comforting images of his childhood: coming in from school on dark winter evenings, his mother at the kitchen window waiting just for him, always with a smile, always with a hug. He desperately needed to see her again as a vibrant living being: the feel of her warmth, her laughter, her smell. The more he struggled, the more he could only visualise the stony grey monstrosity in the living room that he then helped lower into the darkness of the earth. Now they were back in the house and the party was in grotesque, alcohol-fuelled swing. He needed to escape. He took to his mother's bed.

The creaking of the floorboards punctured the silence as Tom entered the room.

'Sorry about not coming to your rescue earlier, Cormac.'

The brothers had shared an eventful afternoon together before Cormac's retreat to the sanctity of his mother's bed. Old Mrs Hopkins, who always hated their mother, a feeling that was wholeheartedly reciprocated, began wailing uncontrollably on the settee in the living room, telling anyone who hadn't escaped immediately how the village would never be the same without Mary O'Reilly. He helped Tom to escort her out of the house. The smell of whisky and pickled onions that set fire to his nostrils as she belched loudly in his face suggested to Cormac that normal service would be resumed after her night's coma. They left Mrs Hopkins, still wailing, on her own identical settee, in her own identical living room, two doors down from his mother's house.

They had barely entered their mother's living room again before Cormac found himself pinned against the door trying to answer a question he'd been asked on at least five occasions that day. It involved 'British Government,' 'Ireland,' and 'ever done.'

He pleaded in vain for help but Tom merely mouthed 'fuck that, brother,' and left him at the mercy of his latest interrogator. Cormac fully understood his brother's reticence.

Tom had attempted to rescue Cormac on the previous occasions only to find himself accosted and accused of being 'a turncoat' like his brother. On the occasion before last, Tom was offered outside by a man he'd never seen before, who only backed down when he reminded him he couldn't be fighting in the front garden on the day of his mother's wake.

'A wake?'

'Yes, a wake!'

'Your mother's wake?'

'Yes, my mother's wake!'

He immediately took his hand off Tom's shirt and transferred it Cormac's.

'And is she his mother, too?'

'Yes, she's his mother too!'

He dropped his hands and looked dejectedly at Tom.

'So I shouldn't be hitting either one of you today, of all days, should I? It wouldn't be right now, would it?'

'No, it wouldn't be right.'

He trudged past Tom to the front door and turned to look at the bewildered brothers. He pointed to Cormac.

'I don't suppose you'll be around on Saturday, by any chance?'

Cormac glanced at Tom, who was shrugging back at him.

'Why's that?'

'Well, it's not every day you get to beat up a British minister. I'm just a bit gutted about it all! So I was thinking I could come back on Saturday and, you know, stick one on you then, if you're around?'

Cormac answered very politely.

'I'm very sorry, but I'll be back in England by then, I'm afraid.'

He turned dejectedly and opened the front door.

'Ah well, not to worry, lads. Thanks for the beer and the spread was lovely. Sorry for your loss.'

And then he was gone.

'Who the hell was that, Tom?'

'Absolutely no idea, brother!'

After the dejected gatecrasher left the premises, his brother promised him he was not getting involved in his battles for the rest of the day. So when his pleading eyes landed on Tom, it was no surprise to him when he merely raised a glass and a smile and mouthed his obscenity. Cormac returned the compliment with his middle finger, before escaping to the safety of the little upstairs room.

He didn't hear Tom walk across the room or feel him sit on the edge of the old bed.

'Fancy a drink, Cormac? There's some food and sandwiches and a wee singsong laid on in Lalor's.'

Cormac didn't respond. He was momentarily lost in his thoughts. He was holding onto his mother's book of prayers. Had she gone through this ritual every night? How many times must she have prayed for him? Had she prayed in vain one day he would once again walk up the path, and wave at her through the window?

'Cormac, we should go to Lalor's. Everyone will be expecting us to.'

Cormac sat up in the bed.

'You know I can't go there, Tom.'

'Why not?'

'Because I'm a British Government minister, and it has been, and always will be, a Republican pub.'

'It's also your mother's wake. Anyway, hasn't anyone told you across the water the war is over? Gerry and Martin are proper politicians now, just like your good self!'

Cormac threw his legs over the side of the bed so he could sit next to his brother.

'Tom, you and I both know as soon as a few drinks have been had, the rebel songs will be belted out and I'm quite sure that won't go down so well with my party or the prime minister.'

'I have a wee idea. I'll put a block on any rebel songs. I'll just tell them it was Mammy's dying wish. What do you say?'

Cormac knew the right thing to do was to spend this time with his family and old friends. He must pay his respects to his mother in the traditional way. That was more important than any delicate political sensibilities. He slapped his brother on the back as they got up to leave the bedroom.

'If I go, Tom, will you promise me something?'

Tom stopped and was eager to ease his brother's obvious concerns.

'Anything brother, what is it?'

Cormac smiled at him.

'Please don't sing "Dirty Old Town", or I'll be forced to call the police and tell them you have been murdering it for years!'

Cormac found himself in a brotherly headlock for the first time in twenty-five years.

As they walked the few doors down and approached the entrance to the old pub, he could feel his stomach tighten. His decision to visit Lalor's was feeling more like a bad idea with every step he took.

—◊—

3

The village of Killane sits nestled in the hills overlooking Belfast. It has a population of approximately five hundred. It consists of one long strip of a main street, at the top of which rests St Peter's Catholic Church and at the bottom, its main competition - Lalor's public house. There are two long rows of terraced houses that stretch from the church until three-quarters of the way down the hill. Two crescents join the end of the terraces and sweep in arcs before meeting again at the end of the village where Lalor's is the first port of call for those arriving from Belfast. Cormac was raised in a council-built terrace that is situated four doors down from the pub and has a clear view of the old church on the hill. There is no school in the village and the children travel by bus to Belfast for their education. The village was and remains 100% conservatively Catholic and 100% radically Republican. The same congregation occupies the educational establishments at both ends of the village. Employment historically was to be found in the farms surrounding the village or in Belfast's heavy industries. Cormac's father had been, until his death, employed at the staunchly Loyalist Harland and Wolf shipyards in East Belfast. He would often entertain the young Cormac with the stories and exploits of his great friends and work colleagues. Cormac never met any of them.

Lalor's pub has been in the village for over 100 years, and has remained in the possession of the same family through all of that period. It is owned by descendants of the original proprietor, John McKee, and takes its name from the 19th century radical Republican writer James Fintan Lalor. In the early eighties, while there was no school in the village, Lalor's was the unofficial political educator of its youngsters. In those days, its front bar consisted of four booths along the right-hand wall and a long bar on the left. Its lounge, at weekends, reverberated to the sounds of Irish music. During the week, it hosted anything from lectures on Irish history, to Gaelic classes, to readings from Irish literature. The room upstairs was where oaths were taken.

A young Cormac sang his first song and drank his first drink in the bar. He danced his first dance and kissed his first girl in the lounge. He spent his last night in Ireland in the room upstairs.

'Come on, Cormac, it'll be all right.'

Cormac and Tom were about to enter the lounge.

'Tom, I'm really sorry, but I don't think I can go in.'

'Half the village is in there to pay respects to Mammy, the other half is on its way! Whatever it is you're feeling, put it to one side for one night and let's give the old girl the send off she deserves!'

Cormac was about to take a step back when he felt a hand slip into his.

'I was looking for a handsome Irishman to escort me. I couldn't find one, so I thought I'd settle for you instead.'

Before he'd time to think, Cormac, Tom and Annie slipped inside Lalor's and found Maggie and Jack's table. Maggie sat alone.

Tom smiled and kissed her on the cheek.

'What would you like to drink, Maggie?'

'Just a Coke, thanks.'

'Sure you don't want a wee Black Bush in that?'

'Tom, you know I don't drink alcohol and besides, I'm going to the retreat tomorrow night.'

Cormac remembered what the argument was about. Maggie had forced her mother's funeral forward so she could go on some bloody retreat! She always seemed to get everything the wrong way round. She was more concerned with an afterlife that may never be than living the life she had. He stifled the urge to continue the argument.

'Maggie, I haven't seen Jack since this morning and even then, he seemed to disappear before we had a chance to speak.'

She didn't look his way.

'Sorry, but he'd some important work to take care of. Anyway, I'm sure you'll see him tomorrow when you all come to my house for lunch.'

Annie pulled up a seat beside her aunt and he marvelled at how much alike they were physically and thankfully how different they would always remain.

Out of the corner of his eye, Cormac caught a glimpse of a huge man marching towards his table. He felt the first pangs of fear since his arrival in Ireland. Why had he listened to Tom? It was a mistake to come here. Why had he come here with no security? Somebody in this place would love to make a name for themselves by battering the life out of a British minister. He was standing above him now. Cormac could feel moisture on his brow. He frantically searched for Tom. The man mumbled something. Cormac couldn't make out what he said.

'I'm sorry, I didn't hear you.'

The big man leaned down over him.

'I said … you got a lot of nerve to say you are my friend!'

Cormac looked up suddenly.

'Dad, are you all right?'

Before Annie had finished, Cormac was on his feet and locked in a warm embrace with the stranger.

'Harry, it's so good to see you. I thought you lived in America?'

The giant let go of him.

'You ain't seen nothing yet. I moved back last year. Too many Americans telling me they're more Irish than me!'

'Harry, before I introduce you to my daughter, will you for goodness' sake stop quoting song lyrics?'

'Sorry … seems to be the hardest word! That's it … I promise … no more … honest!'

Cormac turned to his confused daughter.

'Annie, can I introduce you to Mr Harry Crossan.'

She smiled in recognition.

'Harry Crossan, who you were caught stealing with when you were 11, who got thrown out of your mum's house for bringing a girl back when he was 16, your best friend Harry?'

Harry grabbed her hand.

'Annie, you look spectacular. I've one question for you, though. Did that father of yours not tell you anything nice about me? Or about him and Liam's exploits too, nothing about the three musketeers?'

'He told me you spent half your childhood quoting song lyrics to him and would get annoyed when he always knew the answers.'

Cormac seized the opportunity.

'By the way Harry, in order: Bob Dylan - Positively 4th Street, Bachmann Turner Overdrive -You Ain't Seen Nothing Yet and Elton John - Sorry Seems to be the Hardest Word!'

'You were always a clever bastard, Cormac. Christ, how I've missed you. And now you have Annie, who … fills up my senses like a night in a forest.'

Cormac loosened Harry's grip on Annie's hand.

'John Denver - Annie's Song, and stop flirting with my daughter!'

He spent the rest of the evening with Harry, laughing, arguing and teasing, just as they'd always done. He felt guilty that he might be enjoying his mother's funeral too much. The night ended all too soon with an announcement.

'Ladies and gentlemen, Maggie O'Reilly will now sing for us a tribute to her mammy Mary. Silence, please.'

'When first I saw the love-light in your eyes
I thought the world held naught but joy for me....'

It was his mother's favourite song. She sang it beautifully. It all ended in tears.

—⁂—

4

Cormac awoke, still fully clothed, to the sound of a distant tapping. He opened his eyes and raised his head from the bed. The pounding headache reminded him why he stopped drinking Guinness ten years ago. Annie pushed open the bedroom door and brought him tea and a large glass of water.

'You're an angel.'

She moved to the window, opened the curtains, and unleashed violent sunshine into the room. Cormac pulled the covers over his head. Annie opened the window and he felt the cool morning breeze wash over him.

'Thanks, love, I needed that fresh air.'

'Not as much as I did. The bloody stink in here is appalling!'

Another reason, Cormac remembered, that he'd given up drinking Guinness.

'Oh, by the way, dad, there's a fat man downstairs in an appalling tracksuit, quoting song lyrics, and saying something about you two going jogging this morning. I said I'd get your tracksuit ready for you.'

Cormac peeped over the covers.

'Please tell me you're teasing me, Annie. Harry's not downstairs, is he?'

'No, I'm not! I'm right here, you lazy wee bastard! Now get up and let's go for this jog you promised me.'

Cormac pointed to Harry's yellow and pink attire.

'You were right, Annie. It's a fat man in a ridiculous tracksuit!'

Annie talked through clenched teeth.

'Dad, I didn't say that!'

'Don't be shy, darling. Tell the nice fat man what you said.'

'It's all right, Annie. Your old man is only stalling. Now are you getting up, or what?'

Cormac lifted himself from the bed. He felt his head pounding, his arms aching, and his legs like lead.

'Listen, Harry I'm really sorry, but I don't think I'm capable.'

The relief on the big man's face was obvious.

'OK, then, change of offer. What do you say to a nice bacon and egg soda, cup of strong tea and a gentle walk?'

Cormac's mood lifted.

'I'd say that's a marvellous piece of negotiation on your part. I'll be down in a minute.'

'Appalling!'

'What?'

'Appalling!'

Harry and Cormac looked quizzically towards Annie.

'That is the word I used to describe the smell in your room and that thing that Harry's wearing. Now are you two going for your walk? Because I was thinking of going back to bed for an hour or two before we go to Maggie's for lunch.'

'Where are we going, Harry?'

'Oh, I thought we would just stroll out towards the dam. Just like old times.'

'One minor point, Harry. We're not going to rob the Johnsons' orchard, are we?'

'Not this time, my friend. I've still got the welts on my arse from my Da's belt. I wouldn't care, but it was Liam who did it. I just carried the apples.'

'You were an accessory to the crime and guilty, I'm afraid.'

'Jesus, Cormac! Remind me not to call you if I ever need a good defence barrister!'

As they walked, Cormac was staggered by how close the bond remained between them. He felt an instant connection again with Harry. So much had happened since they had last spent any time together. Of 'the three musketeers', Harry was always the sensible one, the calming influence; the voice of reason. Cormac was the thinker, the idealist; the dreamer. Liam was the wild one, always in trouble, always thinking with his fists. The big man spoke with an unusual urgency.

'When are you planning on going back, Cormac?'

'I've got an official function at Hillsborough Castle at the end of the week. Apart from that, I've got two weeks but I think perhaps I might go home sooner. I'll speak to Annie; see what she wants to do. It's a bit strange for me. I've always been really terrified at the thought of spending any time here because of the threats. Now I'm actually here, though, that's not what is bothering me the most. My biggest problem is that I am acutely aware that I've let down so many people: Tom, Maggie, you, Bernadette....'

'Steady on the Catholic guilt, partner! I can't speak for the rest of them. But you never let me down. I was happy that you got out before it destroyed you. Christ,

I missed you. But I was proud of you. I *am* proud of you – my best friend, the Prime minister of Great Britain!'

'Not quite, Harry. Besides, it's not Catholic guilt, it's a fact. Everything and everyone in my life, I left them all behind, and ran away. Do you know how many times I saw my own mother in the last 22 years, Harry? Never! What sort of a man doesn't even see his own mother in all that time?'

'It's not like you didn't have your reasons. We all knew you went out with Liam that night. He ended up in the Maze for God knows how long, but you didn't. He confessed, he said you weren't there. We knew you would have had no part in something like that. You had to get away. You were a frightened little boy, out of your depth, brainwashed by the history of this sad little island. We knew they would never let you come back. What chance did you really have, Cormac? A great-grandfather who died in the GPO in 1916, a brother murdered for no good reason, and the regular brainwashing sessions in Lalor's. You were fucked before you were even born! It was painful for me to watch someone like you get dragged further and further into that shit. I would have loved to have seen more of you over these years, and I thought a thousand times about contacting you, but I just guessed if you needed me, you would find me. Most of all, I was happy that you got out relatively unscathed.'

'The problem is, Harry I didn't get out in time. By the time I did, I was too far gone and they owned me. Now I am home as a stranger to my own family. I've missed so much that I can never get back. Now that the situation has changed, I want to spend more time here.

Get to know who I am and more importantly, accept who I was. Now everything has moved on, I want to make it up to everyone I hurt. I thought I would never be able to come back here without looking over my shoulder every two minutes, but now I'm here, I can see it was an illusion. It was the machinations of a frightened little boy who was still running. I can see now everything has changed and it can never go back. I want my life back, Harry.'

His friend was shaking his head.

'Cormac, I don't know what they've been telling you lot at Westminster, but I don't quite share your utopian vision of current events.'

'I don't understand, Harry. Are you suggesting that nothing has changed?'

'No, of course it has changed. I'm just saying the underlying mistrust and hatred will take another generation or two to truly wither and die. Come and have a look at this.'

The old friends strolled to the edge of the hill and gazed down on the weary streets of Belfast, at the silent giants in the shipyard in the distance, and the Lough shimmering in the morning sun.

'The problem with this place, Cormac, even today, is that two children can be born into families who live a hundred yards apart and it may as well be a million miles. The bit that really pisses me off is the constant lack of willingness to see the other person's point of view. I never understood why the death of a Catholic was any worse than the death of a Protestant.'

'We should be grateful at least the killing has stopped.'

'Yeah, it has for the moment anyway!'

'Come on, Harry, don't be so pessimistic, you can't believe we will ever go back there again?'

'Put it this way, I don't have much confidence in politicians – no offence intended – and I also have my concerns about letting the lunatics out of the asylum without any real attempt at rehabilitating them.'

'The people, the ordinary decent people, will never allow it to happen again!'

'That would be the same people who now vote in their thousands for Sinn Fein on one hand and the DUP on the other. Whatever is happening at the moment can all be lost again if the right circumstances occur. You are not so naïve, Cormac, that you can believe the complexities which have dogged this little island's history are all suddenly made simple now, because a few politicians are suddenly able to sit in the same room as each other!'

Cormac stretched and gazed down the hill.

'Cheers for that, Harry, you've really brightened up my day!'

His friend sighed and blew his cheeks out over the city.

'Don't mention it, my friend, but I'm afraid I've only just started. I came to see you this morning to ask you to go home immediately, or at least get out of Killane! Those lunatics I was referring to have settled around these parts. There is a group of them here who don't accept the IRA is finished. Who see themselves as carrying the torch of Pearse and Tone. Who think the current leadership has betrayed the cause. They're still using the back room in Lalor's for their meetings, for fuck's sake. I just think a British Government minister walking into their laps is too good an opportunity for them to miss.'

'I'm not stupid, Harry. I checked the risks before I came home and was told that these groups were nothing more than relics. They have no popular support and they present no risk at all. Do you think I would have brought Annie here if I felt there was any danger?'

'I'm just saying that some people are still operating under the radar and intelligence is not an exact science. They sometimes get it wrong.'

Cormac was appreciative of his friend's genuine but unnecessary concerns.

'I am grateful for the words of warning, Harry. The thing is, I am only here for a few days to help Tom and Maggie through this and then I'll be nestled in the Northumberland hills having at least given my family a little support - too little, far too late, but better than nothing. On the subject of family, we'd better head back, or Maggie will have another stick to beat me with when I'm late for lunch.'

'Very well, but take this.'

Harry slipped an envelope into Cormac's pocket.

'What is it?'

'It's the address to my house. None of the clowns around here know where it is. I don't want any of them to see it. If they see a house with more than 4 bedrooms, they think the owner's a drug dealer! Besides, it's on the other side of Lisburn, so it may as well be a million miles away from here.'

'How many bedrooms do you have?

'Nine.'

'Christ, Harry! What do you do?'

'I make money, wherever and however I can. Then I spend it whenever and on whatever I want. It's a simple philosophy, but it makes me happy. It's a shame a few more of the idiots around here hadn't followed my lead instead of blowing each other to hell and back.'

As they walked down the hill towards the village, Cormac had a thought.

'I don't think Roisin would be too happy to see me.'

'What happened between you and Bernadette is between you and Bernadette and anyway, Roisin does what the boss tells her, know what I mean?'

'That's not how I remember Roisin, Harry.'

Harry glanced at him sheepishly.

'Yeah, you're right. What I meant to say was Roisin is in New York looking after some business. There's only me and our Claire staying at the house at the minute. We're going to Dublin tomorrow for a few days, so you and Annie can have the run of the house if you fancy it. The offer is there if you want it.'

When they reached his mother's house, Cormac finally found the courage to ask Harry the question he'd wanted to ask from the moment he saw him last night.

'How is Bernadette?'

'Cormac, you're my friend, and God knows it's been great to see you, but I'd like to hang on to my bollocks, and I'm afraid Roisin has promised to remove them slowly and painfully if I discuss anything about her sister with you!'

5

Cormac opened the front door and called to Annie. He walked through the narrow hall and into the kitchen. With coffee in hand, he made his way to the bottom of the stairs and called Annie again. He heard voices coming from the living room. It sounded like someone was in pain. He pushed the door gently.

'Hello?'

He got no reply. He shouted louder.

'Hello?'

Still there was no reply.

Cormac walked gingerly into the middle of the little room until he could see clearly what was producing the awful screeching sound. Annie lay sprawled across the settee, iPod at full volume, squawking along to some unrecognisable dirge. Although already running late for lunch at Maggie's, Cormac took a seat opposite her. He could not resist an opportunity to be in the company of his darling girl. As he sat, he thought of the many times he'd watched her sleeping as a child. He remembered the countless times when she was a little girl when he would deliberately walk a step behind her and take simple pleasure in her mere existence. He was proud that she had grown into the beautiful woman he knew she would always become. She had a wonderful mind, a wicked sense of humour and a caring nature. She opened her eyes.

'Jesus Christ, dad, you scared the life out of me!'

He smiled at her as she leapt from the settee. He raised his arms to her.

'Sorry, pet - I was having such fun listening to your fantastic voice! I did think at one stage of calling the police and telling them there was a murder on in here!'

Annie made her way across the room.

'You'll not be so smug when we're late for Maggie's lunch and then there really will be a murder on! Oh, I almost forgot, someone called for you when you were out.'

His smile faded.

'Who?'

'I dunno, he didn't leave his name.'

'What exactly did he say?'

She was still smiling, oblivious to his concern.

'Exactly?'

'Yes, exactly.'

'OK, he said, 'Awnie, is your Dawdie in!'

He pushed her away and jumped to his feet.

'Annie, this is not funny, did he say anything else?'

'Jesus, keep what's left of your hair on, dad!'

'I'm sorry darling, it's just I wasn't expecting anybody to call. Are you sure he didn't say anything else?'

'He said he'd call back later and it was nice to see me again, which considering I've never been to Ireland before, I did think was a little bit strange.'

Cormac felt his stomach churn and sat on the settee she had vacated.

'What did he look like?'

'About 6 foot tall, with dark hair going grey at the edges, piercing blue eyes, actually come to think of it, apart from the fact that he was about your age and had pockmarks on his cheeks, he was really rather handsome in that Irish unwashed sort of way.'

He wanted to jump from the chair, push her through the door and get out of the house as quickly as he could manage. Instead, he rose calmly to his feet.

'Annie, pack your things - after lunch, we're going to stay at Harry's.'

He was a poor actor and she sensed his obvious distress.

'Is something wrong, Dad?'

Cormac looked calmly into her eyes and allowed the politician in him to ease his daughter's growing fears.

'Nothing's wrong, pet, it's just that Harry's got an 18-year-old daughter, nine bedrooms, nice wine, and a swimming pool.'

She was already on her way through the door.

'Give me a minute, I'll get my stuff!'

As Annie was getting ready, Cormac flitted from room to room, closing windows and doors behind him. His dear old mother had spent the last 40 years of her life in this tiny space. It had once belonged to the council, until his father had proudly bought it 20 years ago. It was once the most familiar place in Cormac's young world.

Annie was ready. He stood in the hallway and tried to store the little place in his memory. He closed the door behind him and knew he would never return. As Annie waited for him in the hire car, he allowed himself one last glance and finally said goodbye to his childhood.

Before he could start the engine, he and Annie had the inevitable argument over which music they would listen to on the journey. She wanted U2; he wanted The Dixie

Chicks. They each secretly liked both. Annie wasn't ready to 'make nice', and so Bono won. It amused Cormac how much Annie loved U2. He was sure it was due to his brainwashing. He had loved U2 and particularly Bono's lyrics since he had plagiarised 'Sunday Bloody Sunday' for an English A-level essay. They had been driving for five minutes towards Belfast before Cormac realised that he was driving in the wrong direction and he didn't actually know where Maggie lived. He was annoyed with himself. How could he not know where his own sister lived? He was forced to call Tom, who arranged to meet him at the Royal Victoria Hospital on the edge of the Falls Road. They arrived at the meeting place before Tom and sat in silence. Cormac watched the people passing in their cars and on foot and sensed the palpable change in atmosphere. This place had once been so full of tensions, of armoured vehicles, of bloody misery. It was somehow different today. People seemed lighter on their feet, to be smiling more, to be happier. Tom knocked on the window and startled him.

'Sorry, Tom, I was just marvelling at how different this place feels'.

His older brother just smiled and shook his head.

'You always were a dreamer, Cormac.'

He was pricked by Tom's condescension. He got out of the car and stood next to him.

'What do you mean?'

'I mean don't scratch the surface too hard!'

It was his turn now.

'Sorry, Tom, are we talking in clichés now?'

'No, clever shite, all I'm saying is there may be no armoured vehicles, and a few barricades have come down, but this place is still full of bitterness and worse still, it's full of nutcases who are still full of bitterness.'

Tom's words, coming so soon after Harry's foreboding, made Cormac feel uncomfortable. He glanced into the car to ensure Annie wasn't listening.

'On the subject of nutcases, Tom, I think Liam Conlon called at mum's house this morning.'

He looked both ways before answering.

'Tell me you're joking?'

'I wish I was, but from the description Annie gave me, I'm pretty sure it was him.'

Tom took Cormac's arm and pulled him closer.

'If you're pretty sure it was him, what the fuck are you still doing here? He is king fucking nutcase!'

'I didn't want to scare Annie, so my intention is to have lunch at Maggie's, stay at Harry's tonight and get out of here in the morning.'

He followed Tom back up the hill through Killane and onto Maggie's cottage. He checked his rear view mirror several times just in case and was sure that no one was following. He was right. No one was following. No one was following because they already knew were he was headed.

—ɯɯ—

6

It was a little after three in the afternoon when the tall man shuffled around the corner. He walked unsteadily along the derelict street, his home since his release on licence as part of the agreement struck by the traitors on Good Friday. His house was a small two-bedroom box at the end of a row of six identical units. The last of his neighbours had moved out just over a year ago, which meant that apart from his daily visit to the club on the street behind and weekly trek into town to see his probation officer, he could have been invisible. But he wasn't invisible! He was a leader of men! Not many men at this present time; four to be precise. When he walked in the room, they sat up straight. When he talked, they listened. And when he had a plan, they executed it without question. And after three years of working on it, he had a plan; one that had fallen right into his lap. It was not flawless and time was against him. But he knew it was a plan that would shape an entire nation's destiny. It would jolt his people out of their sleepwalk to oblivion. It would place him firmly in the pantheon of great Irish patriots. Throughout its eight hundred years of usurpation, time and time again the Irish people had risen and fought for their freedom. And now in his time, their leaders had let them down. Cast their dreams aside. Sold them a promise of United Ireland based on a lie.

He would not be bought by fancy political posturing, or by the wording of some clever draughtsmen in Whitehall. A few Irish place names, a passport, and a promise of a tomorrow he'd never share was not nearly enough. Platitudes spewed from the smiling mouth of a British prime minister or a former comrade, who'd lost his stomach for the fight, didn't change the one irrefutable fact he knew to be true: he'd been born under British occupation. He'd lived his life governed by British justice, and if the status quo remained the same he'd die under British rule. History had shown, in the darker times, and these were the darkest of all times, it was the actions of a few that awakened the masses. The wolf in sheep's clothing that was the current British administration would bare its teeth again if his plan came to fruition. It would bring the full force of its might down on his people. It had always cruelly done so in the past. As sure as night followed day, it would do so again. And when it did, it would awaken his people from their slumbers; remove the scales from their eyes. He knew he would not be popular. He was not seeking popularity. He knew he'd be reviled by his own people. He knew he might die. A blood sacrifice was a noble act. He knew if he did not die, he'd spend the rest of his life in incarceration. But better to die fighting for freedom than live his life on his knees! History would be kind to him. Future generations would rejoice at his name! They would understand the necessary brutality of his deeds. Just as Yeats recognised the 'terrible beauty' born in Easter 1916, so, too, others would understand the bloody necessity of his actions.

He stopped to take a swig from the cheap vodka he liked to buy on his way home to help him through the nights where he wasn't intending to go back to the club or to chair a meeting with his team. He couldn't go back to the club tonight because he'd been barred. He cursed himself for allowing the rage to get the better of him. It was a sign of weakness. Great leaders of men, truly great leaders, must demonstrate control. The harmless half-wit at the club meant no harm when he laughed at him. After all, he was a fucking simpleton and laughing was all he ever did. No, the poor half-wit just picked the wrong moment to laugh at the missed 'pot'. Before he had time to calm himself, the rage battered the half-wit five times with the butt of the cue on each side of his head. He wobbled like a Weeble before eventually falling onto a pint glass, which took his eye out of the socket. If he was honest with himself, it was worth getting barred for the thrill of the beating and the smell of the blood. He'd only be barred for a day. He could always go back tomorrow. No one would miss the half-wit. No one would stop him going back. This was his patch. That was his club. He enjoyed their fear.

No, the half-wit didn't concern him much at all. He was angry with himself, with his human weakness; the same weakness that nearly destroyed him all those years ago. The same weakness he thought had died in prison, only to creep up on him again when she turned fifteen. When he sat in the darkness on a Northumberland hillside and his eyes became increasingly distracted from his target, writing in the study, and instead watched her grow into a woman in the glow of the upstairs room.

He had allowed it to consume him for a brief moment when he watched the young boy undress her and take advantage of her. So he followed him and realised he was nothing more than a flash young footballer who was cheating on her. He was not good enough for her. When he parked his car across the country road, his intention was merely to block the boy's path: to warn him off; to stop him doing that to her. But when he wouldn't listen to reason, the rage made him pay attention. The rage took the pair of tin snips and a baseball bat from the boot of the car. The snips removed the boy's lips; the bat ended his football career.

The weakness came back today when he called at the house. He knew she was alone. He knew Cormac was out. He had watched him walk up the hill with Harry. No, the weakness made him knock on the door. When she answered, he could see she wasn't wearing anything under her top. He could see from her eyes that she liked him. Why wouldn't she? He was a handsome man. A powerful man. A leader of men.

He thought about pushing her back through the door, of taking advantage like the lame footballer with no lips had done. He had said, 'nice to see you again.' That was fucking stupid but she hadn't noticed. He was angry with himself, yes, but now he had a plan; A plan that was bigger than all of them and would make him more famous than Tone or the Martyrs of 1916. She would ensure it worked. If she didn't, then as painful as it was for him, he would kill her!

—〰—

7

She was at the door waiting, all fuss and feathers, when they arrived.

'You're only half an hour late, boys.'

Tom smiled as they made their way up the tidy pathway.

'Good afternoon to you too, Maggie, dinner smells fantastic. What are we having?'

'Burnt steak!'

Tom lifted his sister in his arms and swung her around. Maggie laughed in spite of herself.

'Put me down you, old fool before you do yourself an injury.'

Cormac couldn't help but feel envious of their obvious affection. Maggie's house was exactly as he imagined. Nothing was out of place. It was old fashioned and was stiflingly neat and tidy. She lived here for 10 years as a spinster before marrying Jack five years ago. They had no children and Cormac, although he hated himself for it, was convinced that was a blessing for the children.

After 10 minutes of uncomfortable silence, Cormac noticed Jack's absence.

'Will Jack be joining us, Maggie?'

He felt her unease at his question.

'Err ... he sends his ... Jack sends his apologies, but he got called away at the last minute.'

Cormac couldn't resist inflaming her obvious discomfort.

'I'm beginning to think he's avoiding me!'

He knew it was the wrong thing to say before he finished his sentence. She was already on her feet.

'Who are you to talk about avoiding, you who have avoided your family for 20 years, and how dare you criticise Jack when you don't even know him!'

Tom tried in vain to intervene.

'Come on, Maggie, Cormac didn't mean....'

'Oh, Tom, for Christ's sake, shut up! If you must know, Cormac, Jack doesn't want to be in the same room as someone like you!'

He stood now toe to toe.

'Someone like me? What the hell does that mean?'

She was more than happy to expand.

'Someone who turned his back on his family, who destroyed his own mother, broke any promise he ever made and who betrayed his people!'

Maggie stormed out of the house. The front door rattled loudly in her wake. Tom, Cormac and Annie struggled to fill the uneasy silence. Annie spoke.

'What does she mean you broke promises and betrayed your country?'

Cormac's simmering fury wouldn't let him answer and instead he wandered into Maggie's back garden. He felt Tom's reassuring presence follow him. He tried to diffuse his own anger.

'I thought that went rather well, Tom!'

'She doesn't mean it, you know, Cormac.'

Cormac sat down on a bench in the middle of a perfectly groomed flower patch. His anger betrayed him.

'She deserves a fucking Oscar if she didn't!'

Tom slapped his knee and sat next to him on the groaning plinth and attempted to justify her.

'OK, she meant it … but she is grieving.'

'Thanks Tom, but the trouble is she wasn't grieving last week, or the month before that, or the year before that. She has hated me since I was a child and to tell you the truth, the feeling is mutual.'

Tom stood and began pacing the flowerbed. He came back and crouched in front of Cormac.

'I shouldn't really be telling you this now, or then again, I probably should have told you a long time ago. You must promise me you'll say nothing to Maggie about this.'

He had Cormac's attention.

'OK, go on.'

'No, I want you to promise on Annie's life you won't speak to anyone about this.'

The gravity in Tom's manner had Cormac leaning forward on the bench.

'I promise on Annie's life.'

Tom hesitated, and then spoke to the flowers.

When you were very little, maybe not even a year old, I can't really remember, Maggie got pregnant.'

'At 13? Tell me you're joking?!'

'Maybe it's best if I talk and you listen.'

'Sorry, Tom.'

'Like I said, she got pregnant, and in those days, in the 60s, it was regarded as not only a terrible sin, but a monumental shame on the whole family. So Mammy and Fr. Mackie sorted it all out between them. I got up one morning and Maggie had disappeared. They organised for her to go and stay with nuns just outside Dublin.'

Cormac stood on the flowers.

'Not a Magdalene laundry?'

Tom pointed to the bench and he sat down again.

'Will you let me finish? She went to a Magdalene laundry and she didn't come back until she was 16 and you were about 4 at the time. Before she went, she was a brilliant girl: bright, funny, and beautiful just like Annie. When she came back, she had completely changed. She rarely smiled, was always tidying, never went out, except to mass. She never saw her baby. Not once. As soon as it was born, it was shipped to America, to some childless family with enough money to pay the nuns. She wasn't even told if it was a boy or a girl. I think you reminded her of what she lost, and you still do. I think when you left and went to England, all the bitterness she buried somehow resurfaced. I know she gave you a hard time as a child, but she was suffering so much. When I look at her, I still see my beautiful little sister and when I swing her around like an old fool, it's the 12-year-old girl that flies through the air. She goes to retreat after retreat, mass after mass, confession after confession, for one reason: to make sure she sees her baby in heaven. I'm not asking you to vote her sister of the year but I suppose I just want you to understand her a little better.'

Cormac was shaking his head.

'Who'd have thought it, Maggie pregnant at 13? Who was her boyfriend? Did dad not kill him?'

Tom started back towards the cottage and spoke quietly.

'No, he just threw him out of the house, Cormac.'

Cormac felt a chill despite the midday sun.

'What?'

'Cormac, it was Daniel! He raped her. It wasn't the first time.'

He staggered the few yards to his front gate. He passed a group of teenagers who were at one stage blocking his way, until he heard one of them say his name with sufficient reverence. He watched them, through tunnel vision, back warily away until they completely disappeared. He enjoyed the moment. As he approached the front door and fumbled for his key, he felt the rage rising again. What if Cormac realised it was him at the door this morning? There was only one thing that cowardly cunt would do. Run! Just like he'd run before. If he ran this time, then the plan was ruined, all because of his unacceptable human weakness. He hoped to be inside before the rage took him, but it was too late. He focused on the pebble dashed wall and swung his fist in an arc. He felt the skin on his knuckles flap from the bones. The vodka worked to dull the pain. But he needed the pain. He deserved the pain for being such a weak cunt! He aimed for the dark patch of blood and skin on the wall. He drew his hand back and threw straight from his shoulder. He felt his bones crack … then nothing … then burning pain. Beautiful, burning pain!

—⚍—

8

Maggie didn't return. They ate the food, which was cooked to perfection. Cormac and Annie said goodbye to Tom and made their way to Harry's place. Cormac's head was so full of Maggie's pain and Liam's menace; he hardly noticed his daughter's growing anxiety. They were on the outskirts of Lisburn before he realised they hadn't spoken since leaving Maggie's house.

'I was thinking, Annie - we might as well go home tomorrow. There's nothing for us here.'

'I thought you had a function to go to at Hillsborough on Friday night?'

'I do, but I'll travel back with the official party on Friday afternoon.'

He felt her hand gently touch his leg.

'There's something wrong, Dad, isn't there?'

He hated himself for lying to her. He had a past she was entitled to know about, but he could never bring himself to tell her the truth. They had always spoken openly about everything, but not that. He pulled the car off the road.

He took her hand.

'I left this place behind me a long time ago. I've built a life for myself and you, and it is so far removed from here, it almost overwhelms me. The trouble is, Annie, there are still people here who won't let me forget.'

She pulled her hand away.

'No, the trouble is, Dad, I don't understand what you're talking about. Let you forget what? What people? All I know is since we arrived in Ireland, you've been on edge. Initially, I put it down to the fact you lost your mother, but it's much more than that. There was that man who called today, and then Maggie's reaction to you in her house. Can't you see these things are incredibly confusing for me? You're my dad, the most important person in my life, the person I love more than anything else in this world. The man I think I know better than anyone else, and yet since we've been here, I have this feeling in the pit of my stomach that perhaps I don't know you at all!'

He could see her lip flutter. He stroked her hair.

'Don't talk like that. You do know me better than anyone else in the world. What I'm with you is who I want to be. To be your dad, to see you grow, to share your life, that's all I ever want.'

The first signs of a tear began to well in her eyes. He brushed her soft cheek with his thumb.

'Please don't be upset. We'll be home tomorrow and all this will just be a fleeting moment in our life.'

She pulled his hand away from her face, opened the car door and began to run. She climbed a fence and waded through the yellow field behind it. He chased her and caught her by the arm.

'Annie, for Christ's sake what are you doing?'

She beat his arm off her.

'What am I doing? I'm trying to understand why my father is still treating me like a 12-year-old girl! Go on, tell me I'm your princess and everything will be OK! Well, everything is not OK. Why have I never been allowed to visit Ireland before? I have a right to know who I am, where I come from, who my family are. We live in a farm in Northumberland, you're a politician, and you're my dad. Who the hell were you before that? Everybody here seems to know more about you than me and more worrying than that, half of them appear to hate your guts! Can you tell me why that is?'

As Cormac held his sobbing girl in his arms, he tried to think of some way of appeasing her without having to return to places he never wanted to visit again. He took the easy option and betrayed his brother's trust. He told her about Maggie. They walked back to the car. She was calm now.

'Thank you for confiding in me. It must have been an unbearable situation for your parents and Maggie. Sorry I behaved like a spoilt brat. I'm the product of a one-parent family after all. That's my defence and I'm sticking to it.'

He entered the living room and was oblivious to the stench of rotting food and stale tobacco. The room was a perfect box. An old second-hand settee wilted under the window. A reading lamp was precariously perched on one end of it. A three-bar electric fire, of which only one bar ever worked, sat sadly opposite. The floor to the left was filled with books which ran the whole length of, and halfway up, the yellowing wall. Great leaders, he recognised, only became great leaders once they truly understood their cause; understood it in a way their followers could never hope to. The books were almost exclusively on Irish history and politics, and included the writings of his heroes. Tone was there. Davis and Young

Ireland were there, Lalor was there, and of course Pearse and Connolly were there.

In the right corner of the room was a 16-inch portable TV. It was there only because he had been given it by someone at the club after he revealed he didn't possess one. It was rarely switched on. He used to like watching Newcastle United on it after he developed a liking for the team through his repeated visits over the last three years. What started out as a 'cover' for his trips soon became a passion. He'd stopped watching recently, in disgust at the irreversible decline that ended in relegation.

He quickly made his way to the kitchen, trailing blood along the sticky carpet.

He opened the two-day old pizza box and inserted its mouldy contents into the microwave. He ran the cold water tap across his mangled hand. He picked up the carving knife which lay in the basin and scraped it across his knuckles to remove any loose pebbles and shards of shattered bone from the open site. He tipped the remains of the vodka bottle into the hole and smiled at the sharp sting. He wrapped his only tea towel tightly around it. He was finished in time for the welcome and familiar ring of his dinner being ready.

After dinner, he settled onto the settee. He tried to keep his mind off her, but she unsettled him. He went back to the kitchen. He rolled the twenty into his nose and vacuumed the powder off the filthy bench. He shuffled to the settee and felt the reassuring buzz fill his head and the familiar stirring in his groin.

He took out his phone and searched the video. Her room lit up the screen. She looked so much younger. He undid his buckle.

—⚏—

9

As Cormac pulled the hire car off the country lane and stopped in front of the imposing wrought iron gates, he took some comfort in the fact they would be safely back home tomorrow. There would be no more awkward questions from Annie. Maggie's pain and his family's shame could be buried under a mountain of work and Liam and the past could remain where they belonged.

Annie was beside the intercom, looking perplexed. Cormac opened the car door.

'What's the problem, pet?'

She raised her hands.

'Harry says I don't know the password.'

'What password?'

Annie beckoned him over. He could hear music coming through the intercom.

> '.... and I would give everything I own,
> give up my life, my heart, my home
> just to have you back again'

Harry's voice came through.

'Well, Annie, did you ask your old Da who sang it?'

She looked at Cormac.

'Tell him Boy George.'

'I already told him that. He wants to know who sang the original.'

Cormac smiled and found himself singing the words, trying to recall the old reggae version of the song. Annie was not so amused.

'Dad, please hurry, I'm wetting myself here. Can't you two continue this nonsense when we get inside?'

'Ken Booth ... tell the smug fat man ... Ken Booth.'

Annie pushed the intercom.

'Dad says Ken Booth. Now please can we come in, I'm wetting myself.'

The gates didn't open. Harry's voice came through instead.

'Tell your old man I want the original artist. His head's been so full of politics and serious stuff, he's losing his grip on pop trivia! It's a bloody tragedy!'

Annie crossed her legs and Cormac took over.

'Nice to see you've grown up after all these years, Harry!'

'Thankfully, there was never any chance of that, my friend. Now stop stalling for time - who sang the original?'

'I don't know ... some 70s bollocks shit crap.'

'That's a fine turn of phrase you possess there, Minister!'

Annie pushed the intercom. 'Harry, could you open the bloody gates or the Minister's daughter will be forced to have a pee on your drive!'

It came to Cormac in a flash.

'Bread, it was Bread ... have some of that, my chubby smug friend.'

The gates still didn't open.

'And the lead singer and songwriter was?'

'For God's sake, Harry ... David Gates. It was David Gates. Now open the bloody gates, will you!'

'You've still got it my friend, welcome to Harry's place.'

As the giant gates swung open to slowly reveal their contents, Cormac and Annie's mouths dropped in unison.

They climbed back into the car and began the journey along the perfectly straight, tree-lined drive to Harry's house, which stood magnificently up ahead of them. Annie managed to close her mouth.

'I feel like Dorothy entering the Emerald Kingdom! What did you say Harry does again, dad?'

Cormac smiled.

'Do you know, pet, I don't actually know, but whatever it is, it certainly pays better than politics!'

As the car came to a halt on the gravel drive, they got their first unobstructed view of the house. It reminded Cormac of an old plantation. There were several steps to the main entrance, which was fronted by four huge pillars. As they approached the front door, Cormac could see the edge of a lake shimmering at the side of the house. He felt enormous pride that Harry Crossan lived here. Growing up in Killane had not been easy for any of them but for Harry, it was torturous. His mother died when he was 10, and he was raised by his alcoholic and frequently violent father. Cormac had lost count of the many occasions Harry would arrive at school with a bruise on his cheek and much worse under his shirt. He often went without lunch - apart from the times when Cormac would pack enough for two. They sometimes skipped the bus home and instead spent the money on chips at the little takeaway at the bottom of the hill. Then they would race up to Killane, trying to get there before the bus returned the other kids from school.

The kids from Belfast were often cruel. Harry's clothes were never clean and his face seldom washed. Harry was always too gentle to fight back. Liam did that for him. While Liam had dreams of revolution and Cormac was full of political ideals, Harry just wanted to make money, to get out of where he was and to move on.

Harry had barely opened the door to reveal the sweeping central staircase which dominated the hallway.

'What can I get you - wine, whiskey, beer, Guinness?'

Cormac was still suffering from last night's indulgence.

'Surely you're joking, Harry, after what we had?'

Harry was in no mood to take no for an answer. After all, he hadn't seen his old friend for over 20 years and God only knew when they would see each other again. Harry convinced him that in the circumstances the only reasonable thing to do was to have a drink together, play some music and end up talking complete nonsense to each other.

Cormac's bowels advised him to choose anything but Guinness, much to Harry's dismay. While Harry was pouring the wine, the kitchen door pushed open. Cormac turned and immediately felt his pulse quicken. *Bernadette?* Before he could speak, she had introduced herself.

'You must be Annie. I'm Claire - very nice to meet you.'

She turned to face Cormac who, even though he realised he was looking at Bernadette's niece, could not disguise his inner turmoil.

'And you're Cormac. I recognize you from the TV. Every time you're on everything stops in this house. I've heard an incredible amount about you from my Mammy and Daddy, and....'

Cormac did not let her finish, but instead took her hand and kissed her cheek.

'You look so much like your mother,' he lied.

'It's funny you should say that, cos most people tell me I'm the double of my auntie Bernadette.'

She had seen straight through him.

His eyes followed her as she approached her father. His pulse would not settle.

'Daddy, did you not offer Annie anything to drink?'

She didn't let him answer.

'Tell you what, Daddy, you and Cormac go and catch up on old times and I'll look after Annie.'

'Good idea love ... but don't you girls drink too much.'

She rolled her eyes.

'For someone who rolled in at God knows what time this morning and has spent most of the day lying on the settee drinking Guinness and watching football ... wouldn't you say you are being a little hypocritical, Daddy?'

Cormac intervened to aid his stricken friend.

'Harry, why don't you show me round the rest of the castle ... I mean house ... and the girls can get to know each other.'

Harry led the way into the living room.

Claire took Annie by the arm.

'Well, Annie, I was thinking you could borrow one of my swimsuits, I'll get the wine and we can spend the evening getting slightly drunk, listening to loud music in the pool or jacuzzi or both. How does that sound?'

'Where do I get the swimsuit?'

Cormac smiled as he heard them scurry away. He was relieved all of her earlier anxiety appeared to have gone.

He was concerned that his own was steadily rising.

—〰—

10

He followed Harry into the opulent living room. It was sparsely, but expensively, decorated by someone with a passion for cream and pastels. His eyes were drawn to a photo gallery which covered the whole of the wall to his left.

'Second row down, far left.'

'What?'

'A picture of Bernie, there's one taken last year, second row down, far left.'

Cormac put on his best frown.

'I was just looking in general at the pictures, Harry.'

'Are you sure you're a politician?'

'What's that supposed to mean?'

'For a career that involves compulsive lying, you're pretty useless at it!'

He raised his hands in mock surrender.

'Point taken.'

As he approached the picture gallery, Cormac was aware of the noisy beating of his heart. It was a familiar feeling to him. One that was present when he stood in the silence of a packed courtroom and was about to address an expectant jury, or was always there whenever he stood in parliament to make his contribution to a debate. He stopped before reaching the wall.

'What are you waiting for?'

Harry was busily strapping his guitar onto his shoulder and hadn't raised his head.

'I can't bring her into the present.'

Harry looked up and sighed.

'You were always too deep for your own good. It's only a photograph, for Christ's sake. Whatever happened Cormac, it was more than 20 years ago. It's all ancient history.'

Cormac moved across the room and sat opposite Harry.

'That's just it. I've spent the last 22 years trying to erase the memory of her, her face, the touch of her hand, the smell of her skin.'

'How much you hurt her?'

There was no malice in his friend's question.

'Yes, that too. But it's more than that, Harry. No matter how hard I've tried to forget her, I don't think a day has gone by when I haven't thought about her. Was she happy? Did she ever marry? Did she have kids?'

'Then why didn't you contact her?'

'Because I betrayed her, Harry. I betrayed her the most. She gave everything she had to me, and I told her she would never regret that. No matter what happened, I would love her, I would never leave her, nothing would ever come between us. Then I ran away.'

Harry tuned his guitar.

'That still doesn't explain why you won't look at a photo that was taken last year.'

'Because the picture I have in my head is of a girl who is forever 18, whose eyes tell me she loves me unconditionally, who has never had her dreams torn to shreds. I am frightened of what I will see in the picture.'

He started to strum.

'I refer the honourable gentleman to the point I made earlier. Too deep! Now shall we play some songs and enjoy what little is left of the evening?'

Cormac picked up the other guitar and followed his lead.

He awoke to the familiar thud of his hangover. As he mustered the will to open his reluctant eyes, he tried to recall the events of the night before. When nothing of any note was forthcoming, he sat up in his bed and peeked into the world. It was only then he realised he hadn't made it from Harry's couch. He stood up in the same clothes he had sat down in and made the familiar promise to himself to be more disciplined with his drinking. Feeling a nausea rising like a rushing tide in his throat, he stumbled to the bathroom and poured the contents of his stomach into the porcelain bowl. He kept his head over the bowl just in case he was not finished. He wiped his mouth with perfumed toilet paper.

'Very classy, Dad!'

Annie stood in the open doorway. Cormac raised a finger to his mouth and whispered to her.

'Shush, pet, we don't want to waken Harry until I've cleaned myself up and at least look like I've made it to bed!'

She whispered back though her grin.

'I think you have a slight problem there, old fella.'

'What do you mean?'

'Harry and some of his relatives, which to me looks like about half the population of Ireland, have just marvelled at how quickly you made it from the living room to here! If I move slightly and you peep around from your strategic position, you might just see a few of them peering this way from the kitchen directly opposite!'

He continued to whisper.

'Tell me you're joking, please.'

She moved to the left.

'I really wish I was.'

Cormac squinted and could just about make out a sea of faces, at varying angles, smiling back at him. He raised his hand to their fascinated gaze and spoke with confidence.

'Good morning!'

He looked at Annie and shouted in a whisper.

'Shit, shit, shit!'

She bent to help him to his feet and whispered back.

'I couldn't have put it better myself, Minister!'

Cormac sat in the silence of an upstairs bedroom. His head felt like someone had reached inside and was intermittently crushing and then shaking his brain. He had drawn the curtains to block the sun's torturous assault on his eyes. As he cringed in the semi-darkness, he made the decision to return to England as soon as his head would let him leave the bedroom and more importantly when his unexpected audience had made their way out of Harry's place. There was a gentle knock at the door and before he could answer, Annie and Harry entered. Annie passed him a glass of water and he gulped it down without a breath. She took the glass and left the room.

'Are you coming down?'

Harry opened the curtains as he spoke. Cormac covered his aching eyes.

'You must be joking! And close the curtains please.'

With the curtains drawn, Harry positioned himself on the edge of the bed next to him.

'Come on down and say a quick hello and I'll get rid of them. They're just curious, what with you being a celebrity and all.'

Cormac opened his eyes to look at the big man, before quickly closing them again.

'Why the hell have you invited half of Ireland here when I'm supposed to be hiding until it's time to leave?'

'It's not half of Ireland; it's my aunt Jean and her kids, and Uncle Pat and his kids. I think Claire told Jean this morning that you were here. The first I knew of it was when they all arrived about ten minutes before your performance in the toilet.'

'For Christ's sake Harry, I'm supposed to be a government minister. How embarrassing is that?'

'Not as embarrassing as them all watching you scratching your bollocks while you slept!'

Cormac opened his eyes.

'Tell me you're joking, please!'

The big man's face cracked.

'Of course I'm joking. Now get over yourself and come down and see some old faces who quite frankly couldn't care less if you are a government minister or the Pope. Well, maybe they would get a wee bit excited if you were the Holy Father!'

Cormac raised himself from the bed.

'Alright, I'll go down there if you make me a promise.'

'Depends what I'm promising.'

'That you will never again use the expression, 'get over yourself'; it makes you sound like a complete tool!'

Harry pulled the quilt off him.

'Point taken, my friend. Now come on.'

—⁓—

11

'That wasn't too bad, was it?'

Harry handed Cormac a mug of hot coffee as he spoke. The last dregs of Harry's relatives had just made their way out of the front door and the two men sat alone in the tranquillity of the kitchen.

'I think it was bad enough. Did you see the look on Jean's face when she was telling her kids about the evils of alcohol?'

'Hey, look, whatever you think, they all came because they wanted to see you and believe me, Jean is very proud of your achievements. I should know, because she's never shut up about them for the past ten years.'

Cormac sat his cup down and studied his old friend.

'What is it?'

'Oh, I don't know. I think it is just seeing all these faces I thought I had long ago forgotten has made me think I missed out on so much over the years. You know, just having people around who truly know you is a special thing. The world in general cares nothing for your soul, Harry. The world I occupy is a pretty superficial place. I had convinced myself I liked it that way. Now I can't shake the feeling I got it all wrong, not only for me but for Annie as well. I think it has been quite lonely for her. I am always away and when

I am home, I am more often than not lost in some document or other. I feel like my whole adult life has been spent trying to escape the present. Does that make sense to you?'

Harry rested his hand on Cormac's leg.

'Yeah, it makes sense, but what you are describing sounds to me like normal life. We all spend our time striving and trying to do the best for ourselves and our kids. Life is hard, and we don't have time to sit and contemplate our navel all day. You have provided Annie with a platform to go on and build a great life. I have watched how she is with you and she adores you, as you do her. She doesn't look to me like someone who feels unloved or deprived or lonely. In fact, she looks to be a pretty happy and contented girl. I think your problem is that you're still beating yourself up about the past, when in reality your life is a very successful and full one.'

'Then why do I feel so unhappy?'

'Maybe you just need a few days to recharge your batteries. You've just buried your mother. I think you're being a bit hard on yourself. I have a suggestion - and before I make it, I won't take no for an answer. I'm taking Claire to Dublin this evening for a birthday treat. We're going to see U2 tomorrow. I would like you and Annie to join us. The girls can have the U2 tickets and we'll find somewhere else to go and put the world to rights. Come on, it will do you the world of good to spend some time with your old mate. These opportunities don't come along very often, so what do you say?'

Cormac's first instinct was to say no; to tell him he had to be back in England for some important ministerial work; to get out of Ireland again as quickly as possible. To get back to the familiarity of the life he had created for himself and Annie a long way away from here. Before he could speak, Annie and Claire were through the kitchen door and listening intently to Harry. The girls squealed, and before he could react, Annie flung herself at him and nearly knocked him of his chair.

'That's brilliant. Thanks, dad!'

He looked at Harry, who was grinning now.

'I told you no was not an option!'

'What's it like?'

Annie had already packed and was standing over Cormac as he paced around the suitcase on the bed. It took him so long to recover from drinking these days that he often wondered if it was worth the bother. It clearly was, because he never once considered stopping. His years as a barrister ensured that abstinence was not an option. It was quite normal to find counsel in a local restaurant at lunch sharing a bottle or two of red wine with their opponents whilst the judge sat alone at the next table with his own bottle. He often felt that the rhetoric in court in the afternoon was much livelier for it. On more than one occasion, he had been forced to nudge a colleague whose head had slumped during an opponent's speech or the judge's closing. As for the politicians at Westminster, he often felt they made his legal friends appear rather tame.

'dad!'

Her voice hurt his head.

'What? And stop shouting, I'm right here!'

'Well you were bloody miles away. I was only asking what Dublin was like as a place, though by the expression on your face since we agreed to go, I'm guessing it must be a shit-hole.'

He concentrated on his packing.

'I have only been twice and on both occasions it certainly wasn't a shit-hole, as you so eloquently put it. It is a beautiful and elegant city, full of life, and somewhere that I have often wanted to visit again. It's just that I didn't really agree to go. Harry bullied me into it, and I have lots of other things to be doing rather than traipsing off to Dublin for two days.'

Cormac lifted his head from the suitcase to look at Annie. Her eyes were on the floor and she was slumped against the doorframe. He walked towards her and held her in his arms. When he held her, he was often filled with regret that her mother never got to feel what he felt in these moments. He was also acutely aware of the passing of time and the fact that in a few months, she would be off to university and these precious moments between them would become so scarce. He thought of the times when she was a little girl and he would kneel to take her in his arms and they would go through their daily ritual when he would say 'guess what?' and she would reply, 'you love me!' He would follow up with, 'how do you know?' and an exasperated Annie would reply, 'cos you always tell me!' The memory and, he suspected, the residual alcohol made his eyes sting.

'I really want to go, Dad. Claire is really nice and I've never had the chance to see U2 or Dublin and it would be great for us to spend some time together before I go to university and Harry seems really nice and you two could get to know each other again and....'

'Annie.'

'What?'

'We're going to Dublin ... relax!'

She threw her arms around his neck. He held on tight.

'Annie.'

'What?'

'Guess what?'

—⟋⟍—

12

The journey to Dublin passed in a blur for Cormac, who was grateful for the comfort of Harry's car. He was asleep as soon as the engine fired up and drifted in and out of consciousness for the entire two-hour journey, until they reached the centre of Dublin. When he awoke, he was startled to find a scruffy little man peering in the front passenger window directly above his head. The cocktail of alcohol, stale sweat and smoke emanating from him caused Cormac to wretch and it took all of his powers not to propel the contents of his stomach over Harry's pride and joy.

'Are you all right there, my friend?'

The little man spat at Cormac.

Cormac tucked his chin to his chest and turned his head in a desperate attempt to find fresh air. He spoke through a closed mouth.

'Yes, I'm fine, but who are you?'

'Sure I am Pat Malloy from Tallaght, and who would I be talking to?'

Cormac looked at the little man's face, which resembled an old peach in colour and texture. Attached to the front of it was a thick moustache which was either formerly ginger and was now going grey, or worse it was fully grey but discoloured by the substances it regularly came in contact with.

'I'm Cormac O'Reilly.'

He offered a dirty hand.

'Pleased to meet you, I'm sure, Cormac.'

Cormac felt a sharp stab in his ribs and turned quickly to find Harry leaning across him.

'Now that you two have exchanged pleasantries, do you think you could possibly direct us to the Burlington Hotel? I've been driving around in circles for twenty minutes and apart from helping me identify you as Pat Malloy from Tallaght, sleeping beauty here has been of no great use to me!'

'Oh, so you want directions?'

'Yes, I want directions! Why else would I be stopping you in the street?'

The man rubbed his chin and some of its debris landed on Cormac's face.

'I thought you were stopping to give me a lift home. Then when I didn't recognise you, I thought I would try to put a name to your friend there to see if maybe I could place him. But to tell you the God's honest truth, I've never met a Cormac O'Reilly either, though I do know a Seamus O'Reilly, but I think he moved to England a good few years ago, or was it America?'

He paused and leaned into Cormac.

'Would oul' Seamus be a relative of yours now, Cormac?'

Before Cormac could answer, Harry's hand was across his mouth.

'Look, Pat, he's not related to Seamus O'Reilly, and no, you don't know me either or the two girls here, but we are terribly lost and would be extremely grateful if you could point us in the direction of the Burlington Hotel!'

He lifted his head from Cormac's face. His fragile stomach was grateful.

'Ah, the Burlington! Lovely hotel, bit pricey for my tastes, but I can tell by the car that money won't be a problem for you boys, what? I went to a dinner dance there once and had me a dance with another man's wife. It didn't end well. But sure it was me own fault, know what I mean lads? Sure she was worth the beating!'

Harry pushed the button and the window next to Cormac started to rise.

'Have a good day, Pat.'

Just as Harry finally closed the old man outside the car and locked a little of his smell inside, there was a knock on the window. Harry sighed and pushed the button again. Pat Malloy from Tallaght leaned in far enough for Cormac O'Reilly, no relation to Seamus, to firmly establish that the moustache was indeed fully grey, but was stained orange in the middle, due to some foreign particles that had not had the good fortune to have met with a bar of soap for some time. He could hold them no longer. The contents of Cormac's stomach left him for the second time in one day.

Undeterred by Cormac's rude interruption, Pat ploughed on.

'The Burlington is on the south side of the Liffey. We are currently on the north side. Therefore you need to be on the south side. Oh, and Cormac here is not very well, so you shouldn't be wasting any more time sitting here gassing with me. I bid you good day, gentlemen and lovely ladies in the back there!'

With that, Pat Malloy from Tallaght walked approximately five paces and disappeared through the door of a semi-derelict public house that Cormac suspected stole his life away a long time ago. Harry passed Cormac a pack of handkerchiefs.

'Well, south of the Liffey it is, then!'

They eventually found their way to the hotel, but not before another couple of surreal encounters with the good people of Dublin. Much to Harry's amusement, Cormac, who had gotten out of the car, was in the process of receiving detailed directions from a young man he had described as 'looking like a very sensible young fella,' when the man in question suddenly stopped mid-sentence.

'Are you in a car?'

After Cormac had pointed towards where the others sat, the man simply scratched his head.

'Ah, now, I wish you had told me that before I started, because I could only direct you if you were walking, you see! I don't drive in the city centre myself, it's a fecking nightmare!'

One final encounter, between a confused deaf man and an irate Harry, convinced them they should pay for a taxi and follow behind. Much to Harry's chagrin, it was obvious to them all they had driven within touching distance of the hotel on at least four occasions.

Harry booked two twin rooms after it was established that the girls, despite having only met the day before, were more than happy to share. They parted in reception, with the intention to meet in the cosy-looking hotel bar. It was not a plan Cormac was universally content with. The thought of a hot bath and climbing into bed appeared a better idea entirely and was overridden only by the pleas of Annie and the pressing need to take some calories on board after the excesses of last night and the inability to retain the contents of his stomach today.

The shower was hot and healing, so much so he only thought about getting out when Harry threatened to evacuate his bowels while chatting beside him. A fresh shirt and ten minutes later, Cormac felt the best he had since returning to Ireland. He reminded himself it had all been self-inflicted and he would have nothing more than a glass of water with his dinner and furthermore at the most reasonable time he could, he would make his excuses and he would be tucked up in bed while the others continued to abuse their bodies. First thing in the morning he would be out jogging the streets of Dublin. Cormac loved to run. The only days he didn't do so were those, like today, when his hangover dictated he would rather do anything else but run. It struck him as another very good reason why he should abstain from alcohol.

'Are we ready for a big night in Dublin, my friend? I was thinking we could lose the girls, get ourselves into Temple Bar, skip eating, partake in nine or ten pints of Dublin's finest, and then a quick 'Abrakababra' on the way home. What do you say, eh?'

Cormac's stomach danced at the thought.

'I was thinking more along the lines of a quiet bite to eat in the hotel and then bed ready for a big day tomorrow. You know, visiting a few landmarks, doing the old tourist bit.'

Harry was splashing aftershave over his chin and shirt.

'OK. Why don't we compromise?'

'What do you suggest?

'Well, the girls want to have a bite to eat with us and then head off into town. Why don't we eat with them and the two of us will take a little walk to Baggot Street and have a wee drink in O'Donohue's, where there's bound to be a music session. One or two pints and if you're not up to it, home to bed it is.'

Cormac felt a surge of relief.

'That sounds a better idea, Harry.'

Harry bent to take the key and his wallet off the table.

'I think I should have been the barrister, my friend.'

'What makes you say that?'

'Looking at the state of you when we arrived, I thought there would be no chance of getting you out of the hotel at all. But by throwing the old Temple Bar, ten pints, and a kebab at you, I got you to agree to what I wanted in the first place, which was a couple of pints in O'Donohue's! Oh I'm good, I know!'

Cormac knew when he had been outdone in a negotiation. He smiled and slapped Harry on the back as they left the room.

'Harry, I'd forgotten what a complete dick you can be, but I have to say you are very good at it.'

'Is that a compliment?'

'I'm not sure!'

They walked to the lift. Cormac enjoyed the triviality of it all.

—◆—

13

The waitress arrived at their booth in the corner of the bar before the girls had made it downstairs. Cormac had already established he would be having a glass of sparkling water and a chicken salad, chosen not because he wanted either, but because he decided they were the healthiest choices on the menu. She asked for Harry's order first, and working from a different set of criteria than Cormac, he ordered a pint of Harp lager, cheeseburger and fries with a side order of onion rings. The waitress spoke to Cormac in a thick accent that must have been Polish.

'And you, Sir, what will you be having?'

He meant to say *a sparkling water and a chicken salad and no mayonnaise, thanks*. But it came out as,

'Same as him, thanks. Yes, I'll have the onion rings as well!'

'I thought you were having a chicken salad, my friend?'

'I was, until....'

Cormac stopped speaking as the girls approached the table. Annie was walking in front, and with her long red hair falling onto her shoulders, she looked as she always had to Cormac, a vision of natural beauty. It wasn't Annie that caused him to stop, though. It was Claire, walking absentmindedly behind her.

She was perhaps a year older than when he had last seen Bernadette. He wasn't sure if his mind was playing tricks on him, but she could have been Bernadette walking towards him. She looked every inch a typical Irish beauty. She had long black hair that framed a delicate pale face. But rather than the customary blue eyes, she had large hazel ovals that dominated her face.

His mind raced back to the early days of his courtship with Bernadette, when late at night, alone in his room, he would listen to Radio Luxembourg, on an old cassette radio held together with a rubber band, since he had broken the mechanism in an attempt to throw it under the bed when he heard his father's footsteps on the creaky floorboards outside his door one evening. It was on that old cassette he taped Van Morrison for Bernadette.

For a year, he was convinced old Van must have written 'Brown Eyed Girl' just for her. He thought he was playing her an undiscovered masterpiece. He would later laugh at the thought of the thousands of brown-eyed girls all over the world, both before and since, who'd had that song played for them. He would often long for the innocence of his early conviction.

'dad.'

'dad!'

'What?'

'Move round the table so I can sit down. And for God's sake, stop staring at Claire. You are making her feel uncomfortable and you are embarrassing me!'

'I'm sorry, it's just … oh, it doesn't matter. What would you like to drink, love?'

Annie and Claire squeezed into the small booth beside them. As soon as they had sat down, the Polish waitress was back.

'Would you like a few moments?'

Annie spoke.

'No, thanks, I'll order now. Could I please have a glass of sparkling water and a plain chicken salad?'

'And you, Madame?'

'The same, thanks.'

It made Cormac smile.

As Claire spoke, Cormac, despite his daughter's chastisement, took the opportunity to study her face in detail, and there was no doubt that his mind was not playing tricks: she really did bear an uncanny resemblance to Bernadette. He felt a surge of regret for what might have been.

'You haven't spoken to Mammy in three days.'

Claire was peering into her father's face as he rolled a beer mat with great dexterity between his fingers. Cormac suspected Harry had spent many hours, in countless bars, perfecting his technique.

'I've just spoken to her and she didn't even ask how you were. Is everything OK between you two?'

The Polish waitress returning with the water enabled Harry to avoid the answer. The rest of the meal was over in a flurry of text messages between Claire and a group of friends who were also in Dublin for the concert tomorrow night. It was settled that the girls were off to Temple Bar to meet them and all that remained was for Cormac to give Annie 200 Euros.

'Ah, Euros!'

Before he had time to explain, Harry had passed over 300 from a huge wad he had drawn from his wallet. Annie kissed Cormac's head and headed off into the Dublin night. As his eyes escorted them to the door, Cormac envied their youth and the promise it held.

'Thanks, Harry, I'll pay you back when we get to a cash point.'

'Don't worry my, friend; it's the one thing I've plenty of!'

Cormac was struck by the thought that, although over the years, word had filtered to him Harry had done well for himself, he had no idea what his friend's line of work was.

'You never said what your business was?'

'Didn't I?'

'No.'

No response.

'Well, what do you make your money from, Harry?'

'You really want to know?'

'As long as it's not illegal, yes!'

'It's not illegal.'

'Then what is it, for Christ's sake?'

'It's shit!'

'Shit?'

'Yep.'

'What kind of shit?'

'The kind that comes out of your arse!'

'I don't understand?'

'I'm the biggest supplier of toilets in Europe, North America, Asia, Australia and more recently South America, the Indian subcontinent and half of Africa. Crossan is the biggest name in toilets since old Thomas Crapper himself!'

'So you really do make money from shit, then?'

'Yep'

'SHIT!'

'Exactly, my friend!'

The two childhood friends made their way towards O'Donohue's on Baggot Street. Cormac was filled with a nagging regret that he knew so little of the narrative of Harry's life. Claire and Annie barely knew each other, when in other circumstances they would have been like sisters; they so easily could have been cousins. Annie had lived such a lonely childhood and here was Harry, his best friend in the world until the age of 17, who had a daughter the same age. Why couldn't he have confronted his past for the sake of his daughter, for the sake of his friendship with Harry, for Bernadette? The answer troubled him, as it always had. It was straightforward; he had simply been a coward. He sacrificed his adult life and Annie's childhood because he ran away and he was still running.

'She left me.'

Harry's voice snapped him into the present.

'What?'

'That's what you're plucking up the courage to talk to me about isn't it?'

Cormac was angry at his own self-absorption.

'I did wonder why you didn't answer Claire. And you haven't really mentioned Roisin at all these last couple of days.'

'I thought you would have enough on your plate burying you mother, without old Harry Crossan here getting all melancholy on you. You know, I thought we would just have a bit of a laugh like old times and then you might want to come back and visit again. I suppose

I didn't want to scare you off with my misery and all that.'

'Jesus, Harry! Life's not like that. You can't just box off something as big as your wife leaving you, in order to have a good time with an old friend, and then open it back up when you feel like it. What happened? When did she leave?'

The big man sighed and rubbed his hair.

'I left her first.'

'But you went back?'

'For fuck's sake, Cormac, are you telling this story or am I?'

'Sorry, Harry.'

'I didn't physically leave her. I just started to get my priorities wrong. Once the business really took off, I threw my heart and soul into making more and more money. I lost sight of why I was making it. It was all for her, you know. To give her the life I thought she deserved. I wanted to show her that I was good enough for her. It was like a thank you, if you like, for choosing me. I suppose I never truly felt worthy of her, what with my background and all. Oh, on the surface, nothing much changed over the years, but then slowly we just drifted, and before we knew it we weren't on each other's horizons anymore. You know you can be in the same room as someone, the same bed, even, and yet be further away from them than if they were a stranger on a train. She tried, God knows she tried. Booking holidays, special nights just for us, taking time to make time. But all of it I threw in her face. I've lost count of the number of holidays I have cancelled because I was too busy. The nights I ruined because I was too drunk. And then two months ago, she went to our offices in

America, phoned me that night and told me she wasn't coming back.'

'Go and get her. Tell her what you have just told me. She obviously loves you; otherwise she wouldn't have made all the efforts she has.'

'You don't understand, Cormac. She stopped making those efforts *two years* ago and I didn't even notice. There would be no dinner when I got home, so I'd go to the pub and eat there. Some nights she wouldn't be home, so I'd open a bottle and play my guitar. She would book holidays with 'friends,' and I didn't even ask who they were or where she was going. Then she started seeing Marcus, one of our solicitors. Can you believe it? My wife left me for a solicitor called fucking Marcus!!! He's in America with her. They'd been planning it for a year, apparently. On the day she left, I got a call from my lawyer to say she had commenced divorce proceedings. So now, my friend, I have all the money that I ever wanted, but no one to share it with. I have a beautiful daughter, who is oblivious to the fact that her parents are separated, because she has gotten so used to her mother's trips abroad, she thinks it's perfectly normal for her to be away for months at a time. The irony of it all is all this time when I thought money was what I wanted more than anything else, I lost the one true thing I needed the most: the love of my Roisin.'

They walked the last few steps in silence.

Harry pulled open the door of O'Donohue's and pushed Cormac into another world.

—⁂—

14

The little pub had a familiar and comfortable feel to Cormac. It resembled the endless bars of Donegal in which Cormac had spent a significant percentage of his childhood holidays. His father, a long-serving and dedicated contributor to the Guinness family fortune, would drag them into the nearest pub within seconds of, and often before, the first spots of rain hit the front windshield of the barely roadworthy car that carried them from Killane every year. Cormac had quickly gone from dreading these regular visits to the pubs of Donegal to loving every part of the experience. Drinking Cavan cola and eating Tayto crisps until his stomach ached. Listening to the songs and stories of the characters they met along the way. He looked forward to meeting new friends whose fathers were also stalwart contributors to the Guinness fund. He would sit enraptured as his father regaled him with the history and meaning of every song that was sung. There was always the occasional old storyteller who could hold the audience transfixed for the price of a glass of whiskey or strong beer. The highlight of every visit was always his 'apparently' reluctant father's rendition of 'Dirty Old Town,' in which he did his best impression of Luke Kelly himself and always, at least it appeared to the young Cormac, got the loudest applause of the day. His more recent experiences of pubs had either been the Members' bar at Westminster or the deserted old place next to his home in Northumberland, where he and Annie would have dinner twice a week with only the disinterested landlord and a neighbouring alcoholic and pungent smelling farmer for company. It was often shut by 9:30 p.m.

This little pub was different. Cormac looked at his watch. It told him it was a little after 10 o' clock. There was a gentle hum of lively conversation punctuated by the occasional sound of a guitar being tuned and what he hoped were pipes being readied. It was nothing more than a narrow track, mirrors and memorabilia along the left side of the single lane and a well-stocked bar on the right. At the entrance was an alcove that was crammed full of patrons who, at a glance, looked more middle-class, dressed down Dubliners than nostalgia-fuelled American tourists. Enclosed behind them were the various musicians that Cormac hoped had not just finished their session for the evening. He followed Harry to the bar, which was thankfully less populated. They found two stools and Harry ordered two pints of Guinness and started into an easy rhythm of conversation with the young barman, while they waited for their drinks to settle. Despite speaking for a living for most of his adult life, Cormac had never mastered the art of idle conversation, and on many an excruciating occasion, had spent a whole evening at some function or other in stunted silence, unable to make a connection with anyone else in the room. He envied Harry his ability to talk for talking's sake. He listened in the hope of learning Harry's art.

'So who's playing tonight, then?'

'It's the Trinity lot.'

'Oh yes, I've heard them before. They're the lot with the uilleann pipe fella and the two good singers, aren't they?'

'That's the ones.'

'Are they both singing tonight?'

'Ah, to tell you the truth, I'm not sure. I heard the girl a little while ago, not sure about the fella. It is all a bit diddly dee for me, I'm afraid!'

'You're working in the wrong pub if you don't like diddly dee!'

'Tell me about it. Have you tried living in Dublin on a student budget? There you go gentlemen, two pints lovingly cared for. Can I get you anything else?'

Cormac thought it was time he joined the conversation, in the interest of politeness.

'You wouldn't happen to sell Tayto crisps?'

'Are you joking? That's all we sell!'

'It would be a shame not to try them, then!'

He could feel the stomach ache coming on before he opened his first packet.

After Harry made it clear that he no longer wished to dwell on his dying marriage, they spent the rest of the evening quietly listening to, and in Cormac's case loving, the diddly dee music. The silence was only punctuated at the beginning of each new song, when they would try and outdo each other on pointless trivia related to the latest offering from the band. The more they played, the more grateful he was for the rain in Donegal and his father's devotion to Guinness. To Harry's distress, he was no match for Cormac's misspent youth. The musicians were highly skilled as they played out the soundtrack to his almost forgotten childhood. 'The Lonesome Boatman' was played hauntingly on the pipes to a hushed audience.

The beautiful poetry of 'Raglan Road' and Cormac's third pint of Guinness made him bite on his lip. The unmistakable introduction to the penultimate song of the night ensured he took the trivia title for the evening with a resounding hat trick of 'Dirty Old Town', Ewan McColl and Salford. Poor old Harry never stood a chance. He was still basking in his glory and enjoying his friend's misery when the girl started to sing.

'I skimmed across black water without once submerging
Unto the banks of an urban morning
That hungers the first light, much, much more
than the mountains ever do.
And she like a ghost beside me
goes down with the ease of a dolphin
And emerges unlearned unshamed unharmed...'

'Are you alright, Cormac?'

Harry was staring straight at him.

'Yeah, I'm absolutely fine, why?'

'Well, it's just that you have tears running down your cheeks and the two attractive women to your left are beginning to stare. What with our knees touching and all, I'm a bit worried you're damaging my reputation and affecting my chances now I'm a single man again!'

'Sorry, Harry. It's just that song was one of my mum's favourites. She sent it to me on an album a few years back. I think it was Christy Moore or it could have been Mary Black, I can't remember. She used to send me stuff you know, on birthdays and at Christmas - music, books, clothes and other things. It was always something Irish. I think she was afraid I'd lose my Irishness or something. I was just thinking how much I loved that song and

I never did tell her how much I loved those presents. I bet she thought I just discarded them, but I didn't. I wore the jumpers, no matter how ridiculous. I read the books. I listened to the music. Sometimes it felt like they were the only things in my life that were real. The rest was just a game, but someday I could go back and start again with my proper life.'

'You can't half belt out a good tune, my girl!'

Harry was no longer paying attention and was instead throwing his arms around a woman who had wedged herself between them. She had some sort of beret on her head and was dressed in some ethnic looking blouse/dress. She wore black leggings, big boots, and a giant scarf wrapped around her neck. As he was all too often prone to do when confronted with strangers, and even though he disliked himself immensely for it, Cormac labelled the intruder. In this instance his labels of choice were: vegetarian, art school, lesbian, middle-class, schoolteacher, protestor, and communist.

She was laughing with Harry.

'You are biased, Harry Crossan. Are you here on your own?'

Harry let go of her.

'Oh, forgive my rudeness. I'm here with my good friend Cormac.'

She turned to face him and before she could speak, Cormac instinctively reached for her hand. He looked at her face for the first time and felt his heart leap into his throat and then bounce to his boots. The eyes were unmistakable.

'Bernadette?'

—⁊⁊—

15

Her hand was gone before he'd finished saying her name. She spun towards Harry.

'What are you playing at, bringing him here?'

Harry didn't seem at all concerned. He sipped his Guinness.

'We're in Dublin for a couple of days. You know I always come here to hear you sing when I can!'

She seemed very concerned. She grabbed his Guinness and slammed it onto the bar.

'And you know I would have no desire to see him! Our Roisin will kill you for this. And I hope she does!'

He picked it up again and wiped the bar with a napkin.

'Look Bernadette, calm yourself down. I'm free to bring him to any pub in Dublin. I don't have to ask your permission. This is my favourite pub, you are my favourite singer and your sister has more important things on her mind.'

Her tone changed.

'What things? She's not ill, is she?'

'No she's not ill.'

'Ah hello ... I'm still here!'

As soon as he said it Cormac knew in the circumstances it was a poor turn of phrase.

Bernadette turned her head towards him.

'No, Cormac, YOU RAN AWAY a lifetime ago!'

He had dreamt of how this conversation would go, if he ever got the chance to have it. He always expected it would be a difficult one, but he naively and secretly hoped part of her would still be pleased to see him after all this time. He thought her justified anger towards him for abandoning her would have been tempered by the passing of time. He hoped other life events would have spread layers of calm over her pain. He studied her and tried to read her face. It was his job, his business, to read faces, to listen for the tone of a voice, to look for clues in other people that would betray their inner feelings. It was a skill he mastered through interrogating hundreds of helpless witnesses in court. A skill he perfected in Parliament. A skill that no matter how much he tried to suppress it, was telling him the woman staring at him was feeling pure and undiluted contempt for him.

His observations forced him to frantically search for something, anything to say that might defuse the awkwardness of the situation.

'I never knew you could sing like that. You are really very good.'

'Thank you.'

He felt a cooling in his temperature. There seemed little hostility in her voice and it settled his nerve, until he sensed she hadn't quite finished.

'I didn't find my voice until after you FUCKED OFF AND LEFT ME!'

He saw Harry wince and felt the need to loosen his collar. The barman and the three men behind Harry reacted to her raised voice and were all staring intently at him.

He was aware of someone standing next to his left shoulder. He turned and was confronted by a tall, bespectacled, cravat-wearing man. He wore a tweed jacket with suede patches on the elbows and was holding a black violin case. He also appeared to be paying far too much attention to their conversation. Cormac, still smarting from Bernadette's assault, felt a sudden urge to pick a fight with an English professor.

'Can I help you, mate?'

'I am not your mate. And no, I very much doubt you can help me in any way!'

His tone smacked of pure condescension. Cormac thought this a very promising sign: the English professor, with the upper-crust Dublin accent, shared his mood for a fight.

'Then why don't you do us all a favour and fuck off from where you came. We're having a private conversation here.'

The professor leaned into Cormac, so he was inches from his left ear.

'I am afraid I won't "fuck off," as you so eloquently put it, because I have rather a vested interest in your conversation.'

Cormac leapt from his stool, which reduced his height disadvantage by about a foot and a half and placed his forehead in a particularly good position to make contact with his opponent's sizable nose.

'Look, what is your fucking problem?'

The tall man removed his spectacles and held his ground.

'My problem, Sir, is you are clearly upsetting my wife!'

His words hit him harder than a punch. Cormac's knees forgot their function and he fell back onto the stool.

'It's alright, Peter, he's an old friend of Harry's. You pack up the rest of the stuff and I'll be over in a minute.'

Bernadette's intervention diffused her husband's anger and hastened his departure. Cormac spoke to her feet.

'I didn't know you were married.'

'Why would you? It has got fuck all to do with you. So if there is nothing else, I think I'll be off. Give my love to Roisin, Harry.'

She started to move away from him and he instinctively moved his left leg to block her path.

She glared at it.

'Move your leg or I'll shout for Peter and I can tell he already doesn't like you much!'

He knew he couldn't let her go. He didn't know how to make her stay. He needed to think quickly.

'There is something else!'

He didn't know what that 'something else' was.

'What else?'

He blurted out the first thing that came.

'Meet me tomorrow, at the Ha'Penny Bridge at 10 o'clock! Do you know where it is?'

He wasn't sure where it came from or where it was. He had read about it once, in *Ulysses* maybe.

'Move your leg!'

She pushed her knee into his thigh. He didn't let her go.

'Answer me first. Will you come?'

'Move your leg and I'll answer you!'

He moved, so she could position herself where her husband had stood moments before. She leaned in close so he could feel her breath on his ear. It made his chest flutter.

'Yes I know where the Ha'penny Bridge is. Everybody in Dublin knows where it is. As far as me agreeing to meet you there at 10 o' clock tomorrow is concerned, GO FUCK YOURSELF, CORMAC!'

With his ear still ringing, he turned to see the door close behind her.

He looked at Harry, who was sipping his pint and trying unsuccessfully to look nonchalant. Cormac raised his glass to him.

'You are a complete dick, Harry! But thanks for bringing me to her. And not telling me she was married. I wouldn't have come if I'd known.'

'No problem, my friend, and may I say, I thought you handled her and the husband particularly well!'

'Harry.'

'What?'

'Fuck off!'

'Roger that, my friend. Roger that!'

—✦—

16

Harry's gentle snoring had gone from being a source of great annoyance to a comfort for Cormac. He guessed it must be around 4 a.m., but refused to confirm it by checking the red glow emanating from Harry's bedside table. Knowing would guarantee he would never sleep. He had spent many a night in hotel rooms in exasperated amazement at how uncomfortable they could be. He was convinced there must be a sadistic room designer somewhere out there who took sick pleasure in destroying the lives of businessmen and travellers all over the world. The air conditioning was always too noisy. The heating always set too high. And the beds designed for anti- sleep. He'd lost count of the occasions when his legs had kicked their way out of the perfectly folded prison they were trapped in. And the pillows! *Oh God! The fucking pillows!*

The four pints in O'Donohue's would ordinarily have provided the antidote. Seeing Bernadette again had completely negated their effect. He always expected she would be angry and she certainly hadn't disappointed him. But married? Why had he not considered she would be married? Of course she would be married. She was a 40-year-old woman he had deserted as an 18-year-old girl. She was a stranger to him. She'd lived a life he knew nothing about for more than 22 years; a life he had no right to know anything about. After all, he'd married Jill, and there were other relationships along the way, weren't there? He tried to think of them. There was Rachael, an ambitious young barrister, with whom he'd endured two months of torture due to her inability to accept his love for Annie was not something she needed to, or could ever hope to, compete for. There was a divorced journalist called Jane, *or was it June?* Who carried more baggage than an average airport carousel and therefore lasted less than a month. There were uncomfortable dinner dates with two or three others whose names he couldn't, or didn't care to, remember. But mainly there had been Annie and work. Yes, Annie had been his life and work his mistress. But Bernadette, she was entitled to fill her life any way she chose. *Maybe she'd had 5 husbands? 50 lovers? 100, even?* He sat up and switched on his lamp to banish the last thought from his mind.

He looked at Harry, who had obviously found the secret for defeating the hotel anti-sleep brigade. He tried to remember the last time they had shared a room together. His thoughts turned to the day, or night, rather, he became convinced that Harry was to be his best friend, to the exclusion of all others. The night he knew he could trust Harry above anybody else. Until that night, it had always been the three musketeers, Cormac, Harry and Liam. They'd all been selected to attend residential trials for the Belfast District under-11s football team. It was a time of great celebration in Killane.

The village rejoicing was a little premature, as none of them made the team. Harry, who was a goalkeeper, had tight curly hair, and the letters 'PS' especially stitched into his shirt in honour of his hero at the time, Peter Shilton. Unfortunately for Harry, that was where the similarities ended. And in the days before political correctness destroyed the art of the PE teacher put-down, he was told:

'Son, my granny could have done better than you today. And she's been dead a year!'

Cormac was a centre forward who didn't manage to score in any of the four matches played over two days. The boy that was chosen instead of him scored 17; 9 of them in the same match he and Cormac were playing in! Liam, who was a tough tackling midfielder, and had all but been informed he'd been selected, got sent off, and then subsequently sent home, for telling the referee to 'fuck off back to England' after he detected a hint of an accent before the kick off in the final game.

Cormac's abiding memory of the event was that it entailed a one-night stopover at Jordanstown Polytechnic halls of residence. It was to be the first time he'd ever stayed away from home. Like the other boys, he was very excited at the prospect, as it was an obvious indicator he was now a grown up who could stay away from his parents' house for a whole night. The sense of excitement lasted right up until he was shown his room, which was one of six in a hallway with a little kitchen at the end of the corridor. The walls of his room were covered from top to bottom with the most hideous of ghoulish paintings. If his sense of excitement waned at this point, it transformed itself into complete and utter terror after the lights went out at bedtime. He lay staring at the twisted faces on the wall until he convinced himself they were not only moving but closing in all around him. He was sure if he didn't make his move and get out as quickly as he could, he may never be seen alive again! Without attempting to switch the light on, he made a dash for the door, wearing nothing but his new Superman underpants his mother had bought him for the trip. After a moment of blind terror, when he couldn't turn the lock and at the same time he could have sworn he felt a breath against his neck, he was out in the dark corridor. He knocked gently on Harry's door. To his great relief, he heard Harry's footsteps on the other side.

'Who is it?'

'It's me, Cormac.'

'What do you want? Go back to your room, or we'll be sent home.'

'Harry please open the door. I'm really scared.'

And this was the point when Harry Crossan became Cormac O' Reilly's best friend in the world.

Harry opened the door and let him in. He said Cormac could sleep on his bed and he would sleep on the floor. He said anyone would have been scared in that room. He said he would never tell anyone, especially not Liam, that Cormac had been crying.

He never told.

'Are you awake, Harry?'

'Harry?'

'Yes, I'm awake.'

Harry sat up on and placed his pillow behind his head.

'How could I not be awake? Rip Van Fucking Winkle couldn't sleep in the same room as you! I've been awake since you switched the fucking light on! And I was awake about 2 o'clock when your pillow hit the TV and nearly knocked the lamp over! Cormac, it's half-four in the morning. Switch the fucking lamp off, would you?'

'I'm sorry, it's just my mind has been racing since we saw Bernadette. She looked beautiful, didn't she?'

'She's looked beautiful for the last twenty years. So it wasn't exactly a surprise to me.'

'She was pretty angry, though.'

'Yeah, Cormac, I think it is safe to say she was angry, alright.'

'How long has she been married to the English professor?'

Harry got up to go to the bathroom.

'How do you know he's an English professor?

'Is he?'

Harry shouted from the bathroom.

'Yeah, he has a chair at Trinity.'

Cormac congratulated himself.

'How long has she been married?'

'About five years, I think?'

'Is she happy?

Harry climbed back into his bed and pulled the covers over his head. Cormac flicked his lamp off.

'Jesus, Cormac! I don't know if she's happy or not. I couldn't even tell my own wife wasn't happy!'

'Why did you bring me to see her?'

'Because you're my friend and I thought you would want to. Maybe I thought you two still had something to say to each other. I don't know.'

Cormac lay down on his uncomfortable bed.

'Do you think she will come tomorrow?'

'I think it is highly unlikely, my friend.'

'Do you mind if I go, just in case?

'I would expect nothing less.'

'What about Annie and Claire?'

'I'll look after them.'

Cormac felt a sudden need to sleep. He turned on his side to face the window, where the first light of the morning was framing the curtains.

'Thanks for Jordanstown, Harry.'

He didn't answer.

The flicker of hope for the coming day and the comfort of Harry's gentle snoring rocked him to sleep.

—⁓—

17

The pain in his neck ensured he woke early. The four pints of Guinness meant the first minutes of his morning would be a battle between his trainers and his need for breakfast. Despite the noisy pleadings of his stomach, he grabbed his tracksuit from the case and pulled his trainers on. He shut the door gently on his way out and made his way along the corridor. He turned left to the lifts that would take him into the brisk Dublin morning, where a steady forty minutes would set him up nicely for the day.

'Morning, Dad.'

Annie was peeping at him from behind the bulk of a huge man who was about to send the breakfast shift into meltdown.

Her hair was tied in a tight ponytail which showed her fine features to full effect. She rarely used make up and this was one of those occasions where she wore none at all. He liked to see her without make up because he could still make out the last traces of his self-conscious, awkward little girl that would all too soon be gone forever.

He circumnavigated the bulk between them.

'Good morning, love. You look magnificent.'

'One of us has to. You look like shit!'

He turned to see if the big man was showing any interest, but he had already disappeared into the lift and was impatiently holding the door for them.

Cormac signalled for him to descend without them.

'You know I don't sleep very well in hotels. Anyway, I am 40 – I'm supposed to look like shit in the mornings.'

'It's good you are going for a run, though. You haven't run for over a week.'

'You sound like my personal trainer.'

'It's not that. I just like to see you get some exercise because your diet is crap.'

'My diet is not all bad. If anything I would say I am a bit of a 'yo-yo' dieter.'

'Yeah – unfortunately, the only 'yo-yos' in your diet are the mint flavoured ones you dunk in your coffee!'

'Annie, has anyone ever told you that you are a comedian?'

'No.'

'Did you ever think that might be because you are not very funny?'

By the time he walked her to the breakfast restaurant, the four pints of Guinness had come up on the blind side of his trainers and stormed into an unassailable lead. He told himself he would definitely run tomorrow and in view of what Annie had said about his diet, he would join her and outmanoeuvre her on the healthy breakfast stakes.

The young Polish waitress from last night met them at the door and showed them to a table next to the window. It was adjacent to their friend from the lift, who was idly reading the *Wall Street Journal*, but paying considerably more attention to the thick beef sausage on the end of his fork. This only reinforced Cormac's desire to start the day with a healthy choice. The Polish waitress was back at their table and it seemed to Cormac she was now doing a more than passable impression of Tom Conti's character in *Local Hero*: a quirky little film he'd enjoyed a few years previously where Conti was the pub landlord, postmaster, and just about everything else in his little village.

'Madame?'

'Fruit juice, poached eggs and wholemeal toast, please.'

He looked up at Annie. *Good choice, but not nearly good enough!* She had clearly left the 'iced water and muesli' door ajar for him to claim the smug healthy breakfast trophy for today!

'And Sir will be having the full Irish breakfast?'

'Ah … yes… err… that would be lovely. It's not every day you get your … ah… breakfast cooked for you. Is it now? Best to make the most of it!'

He felt the first twinges of his defeat.

'And Sir will be having black pudding and fried bread with that?'

'Sure, why not? You only live once, isn't that right?'

The Polish waitress was already gone, presumably to cook the breakfast, make up the rooms, and do the accounts before her afternoon shift started. He flicked a guilty glance at Annie. *Was she shaking her head or just fixing her hair?* His friend to his left raised half a sausage as a toast to him.

His trainers suddenly felt uncomfortably tight.

He could see Tom Conti, carrying his heart attack, fast approaching from behind Annie's shoulder, so he thought it best to distract her to stave off the lecture at least until he had satisfied a little of his raging hunger.

'So, how was your night last night, pet?'

'Do you know what Dad? I had a brilliant time. I am so pleased we came. Claire is lovely and her friends made me really welcome. I felt like I had known them all my life. Mind you, I think the ten triple vodkas and cranberry juice helped!'

Cormac dropped his fork.

'Annie, that is so dangerous, and so unnecessary. Do you realise the damage that can do to you?'

She looked up at him and smiled.

'Relax, Granddad. I'm only messing with you. I didn't have any alcohol. I wanted you to feel like I do when I see you shove crap in your mouth on a regular basis.'

He pushed his plate away.

'Point taken!'

'No, seriously though, I had a fantastic time and I am so excited to be going to see U2 tonight. After all the brainwashing I was subjected to as a child, it will be great to see what all the fuss was about. We're meeting Claire's friends about 6 o'clock. So I'm really looking forward to spending the day with this rather handsome, if slightly chubby older man, who might take me shopping and then for some nice lunch just to make it the perfect day!'

'Ah!'

'By the look on your face, and the fact that you seem to have lost the power to speak, I sense that taking me out for the day doesn't quite fit in with your plans?'

'Oh, I'm sorry, love, I know you were looking forward to us spending some time together and believe me, I was too, and in any other circumstances, you know I....'

'Dad, just spit it out, would you?'

'I met someone I haven't seen for a long time last night and I am sort of hoping I can get to spend more time with her today.'

'Her? Who's her? Have you got a date?'

'Her is Bernadette, and I wouldn't call it a date exactly.'

'Bernadette! *The* Bernadette?'

'What do you mean *The* Bernadette?'

'Oh come on Dad. *The* Bernadette, no one has shut up about since we came home? *The* Bernadette, Claire never stopped talking about last night? *The* Bernadette, you abandoned when you mysteriously disappeared to England leaving her heartbroken? The same Bernadette I didn't know existed until three days ago!'

'Yes, that Bernadette. And I am sorry I never told you about her. It was just she was part of another time and place I never wanted to return to.'

'So why do you want to now?'

'I don't know. The time is right for me to stop running. I am tired of running.'

He felt her hand on top of his.

'I don't understand, Dad. What are you running from?'

He placed his other hand on top of hers.

'Annie, I've already said too much. I need you to trust me. When the time is right, I will tell you everything. Will you bear with me a little bit longer? I'm sorry.'

She stood up and moved around the table to him and he rose to meet her embrace.

'Just for the record, from my ill-informed position, I'm glad you have a date with Bernadette. You deserve to be happy and if you're happy, then so am I.'

'It's not a date.'

'Why not?'

'Because she hasn't said she will turn up!'

'Do you think she will?'

'I really hope so.'

'Well it's a potential date. And if she turns up, then it's a real date!'

He pulled away from her and found his seat.

'Not quite?'

'Why not?'

'She hates me. And, oh yeah ... she's married!'

She moved behind him and placed her arms around his shoulders.

'What a pisser!'

'Not sure if I completely approve of your language, but my sentiments entirely!'

—⟩⟩⟩—

18

Cormac stepped into the bright sunshine of a Dublin morning. He made his way along the Georgian street, nestled beneath a clear blue canvas. He was wearing yesterday's clothes and a jacket borrowed from Harry. The jacket was necessary to cover the stains of last night's Guinness. It was at least two sizes too big, but was more than adequate for its purpose. He had some faith the concierge's directions would prove to be more accurate than Pat Malloy from Tallaght's had been. Nevertheless, he set out fifteen minutes early, partly due to his general lack of confidence in the Dublin population's navigational capabilities, but more because he was too excited to stay still. He needed to be moving towards her.

Two events slowed his journey, but not enough to make him late. He stopped to rescue a distressed jogger who was being pinned against the beautiful red door of a Georgian terrace by an ugly black Rottweiler. Cormac, as a regular jogger, had acted the man's part in this scene on too many occasions to remember. The dog owner, who was nearly, but not quite as big as her dog and maybe two stones lighter, was treating the exercise as a test of her handling skills. She was failing! It was clear to Cormac that she was oblivious to the sheer terror evident on the skinny man's face.

As Cormac approached the scene, the well dressed old lady was observing the dance between her beast and the frightened man.

'Come on, Poppet. Stop this silliness. The bad man scared you, I know. Running up on you like that! He frightened you didn't he, my pet? Sit, Poppet, sit!'

Poppet was not in the mood to sit. In fact, Poppet looked like she was about to remove a sizeable portion of the jogger's left leg! The old lady was offering little comfort.

'It's alright; she's more frightened of you than you are of her.'

The ghostly pleading face that stared at Cormac made a lie of that observation.

'Please, mate, get it off me! Just get it off me! Please!'

Cormac turned to the four-foot handler, who he estimated to be seventy-five at the youngest and maybe ten years older. The gentle old lady was now pleasantly smiling at him while idly swinging a large chain lead.

'Excuse me, but could you not put the dog on the lead? I think it is going to bite him. Can't you see that he is terrified?'

The smile was gone.

'Where are you from, son? England, is it?'

The tone was pleasant, friendly even.

'What's that got to do with anything?'

'Oh, I just couldn't place your accent.'

Poppet's continued grunting and growling suggested she wasn't too bothered about anything else on the planet apart from how best to dismember the jogger.

'I live in England, but I'm from Killane.'

'That's in the north, isn't it?'

'Yeah, just outside Belfast.'

And then the rest was a blur. He was sure the chain came first. It caught him on the right ear. Poppet came next and attached herself to Harry's jacket. The jogger became a sprinter. Cormac kicked the dog. The pensioner kicked Cormac. Cormac became a jogger. The pensioner developed Tourette's syndrome. As he was leaving, he heard at least ten 'fucks', five 'bastards,' three 'northerners,' two 'wankers', and one very loud 'CUNT!'

At a safe distance, he looked back to see Poppet sitting obediently and receiving her treat from her devoted old master. His ear throbbed. His arm ached. He was happy that his foot hurt!

As he looked up to recover his bearings, he found himself standing directly in front of a plaque dedicated to the women of the 'Magdalene' laundries. He forgot the pain in his ear, his arm, and his foot. He forgot Bernadette. He mourned for Maggie. For her stolen innocence. For the theft of her childhood. For her lost child. Oh Christ! What kind of pain was that to bear? Poor Maggie, she had suffered intolerable pain at the hands of her own family. Her brother's evil, compounded by her mother's misplaced desire to make it right. He felt guilty for his thoughts of his mother in this the week of her death. And what of Maggie's lost child, now living somewhere in America? A niece or nephew he would never know. But more - an innocent, condemned before its birth to never know the love of a devoted mother. To never know where he or she came from.

He promised himself he would go to see Maggie before he went home. Not to do anything in particular. Just to go and see her for no other reason other than to spend a moment with her without the hatred, the anger, the bitterness. His ear began to throb. His arm ached. He turned and limped towards Bernadette.

He slowed his pace just on the edge of Grafton Street, after the young busker thanked him for his first payment of the day, and told him he was only ten minutes from the bridge. Cormac stayed and listened to the scruffy boy's rather dubious rendition of U2's 'All I Want is You.' He worried for the boy's ability to add to the two Euros he had deposited onto his guitar case. In doing so, Cormac took care to avoid eye contact with the boy's underfed terrier that was showing too much interest in Harry's jacket for his liking. By the time he had reached the end of Grafton Street at 9:45 a.m., he had passed four more U2 impersonators, two very impressive James Joyce's, a man who appeared to be sculpting dogs out of a small mountain of sand, and a transvestite on stilts. Cormac began to feel Dublin was a city he would like to visit more often. As he passed Molly Malone and Trinity College, his doubts turned to certainty that she would not be there to meet him. After all, why should she? How arrogantly deluded was he to think he could just turn up in her life like that? Threaten her husband in a pub, and then ask her to drop everything to come and meet him? Most definitely she would have had plans for today. Work, even. In his eagerness to see her, he had said 10 o'clock. Wouldn't it have been more sensible to arrange a time in the evening when she might just be free? Had he even stipulated that it was 10 in the morning and not the evening? By the time he reached the Ha'Penny Bridge with five minutes to spare, he was absolutely convinced he was in for a long wait, and even then, it was unlikely she would turn up tonight!

She was there waiting for him.

—⁓—

19

On O'Connell Bridge, just downstream, a man with a bandaged hand watched Cormac check his reflection in the shop window. It was a risk to be so close, but it was one he had been taking for such a long time, it had become as necessary as breathing for him. He wished he could have stayed longer, but he had an appointment to keep. The 'Chemist' did not like to be kept waiting. Besides, he was eager to see what he could get for his money. He picked up his holdall and melted into the morning throng.

She was leaning over the railings of the bridge. Her arms folded, standing on one leg, with the other tucked in behind her knee. She was gazing into the stillness of the Liffey water. It was a pose he recognised. She was someone who had gotten used to waiting. She hadn't noticed his presence, so he stole a moment just to look at her. It was as if time had been unable to leave its mark on her. Her hair was shorter than when she'd been a girl but longer than he remembered from last night. It hung down over her left eye and was tucked behind her right ear. The clothes she wore, a light business suit, were the only indication that she was not the girl who had smiled shyly at him before agreeing to dance with him at Lalor's all those years ago.

He noticed her sister Roisin at first, who had smiled at him as the group of eight girls entered the old pub. Roisin, of the entire group, caused quite a stir among Killane's finest. She was first through the door and first to ask if any of the open mouths wanted to buy her a drink. Harry Crossan ordered it and was sitting beside her before Bernadette walked in, head bowed, at the back of the group and stood self-consciously behind her sister's back. She focused mainly on the floor, but occasionally peeped out from under her long dark hair. When her eyes settled on Cormac, they set a hammer off in his chest. She remained standing there for the rest of the night. Her eyes fixed on the floor except occasionally when he was sure they were searching for him. He watched in impotent horror, as one after the other, every eligible boy in the room made his way to her. His spirits would rise, as one after one was turned away with a shake of her head and a glance to him.

'They're getting picked up in ten minutes. You better make a move, Romeo.'

Harry had surgically removed his backside from the stool at the bar and his lips from Roisin while she and Bernadette had gone to the bathroom.

'What do you mean, Romeo? You're the one who hasn't left that girl's side all night.'

'And you haven't taken your eyes off her wee sister in the red dress.'

'She is beautiful Harry, but I don't know what to do.'

'What do you mean, you don't know what to do?'

'I've never asked a girl out before. In fact, I have only spoken to about three, and two of them are my cousins and the other one is Maggie, so they don't really count, do they? It's alright for you. You've had loads of girlfriends. '

'I've had three, actually, and two of them were *my* cousins, so they don't count either!'

'Were they?'

'No, of course they fucking weren't. I'm just trying to make you feel better about being such a dick!'

'I'm sorry, Harry. I just wouldn't know what to say to her, and I would just end up making a fool of myself.'

'And don't you think standing at the other side of the room, staring at her all night without saying a word to her, is making a fool of yourself?'

Cormac didn't have time to answer before Roisin and Bernadette reappeared from the bathroom. They walked across the small dance floor before stopping in front of Harry. Roisin stood in front of Bernadette and Harry stood in front of Cormac.

'Harry, here's my number. We're going to wait outside. Our minibus will be here in a minute.'

Then they started to walk away and the room started to spin on its axis. Cormac's hammer started banging in his chest. But still he let her go without a word.

He could hear Harry shouting over the beginning of the last song of the night.

He watched Roisin turn and walk back to Harry. She called Bernadette and spoke into her ear. Bernadette smiled and walked towards Cormac.

'Bernadette, this is Cormac and he would like to ask you to dance.'

Harry kicked him. It didn't hurt.

'Wouldn't you, Cormac?

She was waiting for him to speak. Her arms were folded. She was standing on one leg with the other tucked in behind. Her hair hung down over her left eye and was tucked behind her right ear.

'Yes.'

She took his hand and they walked to the dance floor. They arrived just as the intro was ending:

'A love struck Romeo sings a streetsuss serenade
Layin' everybody low with a love song that he made
Finds a convenient streetlight steps out of the shade
Says something like you and me babe how about it?'

She put her arms around his neck and held on tight, like she never wanted to let him go.

Harry was right. He was Romeo, after all. He had just needed a little help from Mercutio.

Even through the grime of the shop window, he could tell the years had not missed their mark on him. There had been too many late lunches and late nights; a chronic lack of interest in his wardrobe; too much interest in fried food. They had all left him suddenly aware of the paleness and slackness of his face, the uncomfortable tightness of his belt and the ridiculousness of Harry's recently ruined jacket. He resembled a prematurely aged, chubby schoolboy, wearing his older brother's hand me downs a year before he was ready for them. His nerve, which had deserted him, began to make its way back to him, when he reminded himself of last night. *Hadn't she seen him slumped on a bar stool after four pints of Guinness? Hadn't she watched him threaten her husband? Hadn't she told him in no uncertain terms that she was not going to come? Yet come she had. And not only that, she was early! Why would she be here? He felt his confidence return in a flood. There was only one reason: she wanted to see him!*

Free of his momentary stage fright, he made his way onto the quaint old bridge. Any second now, she would look up from the gently flowing water. Her eyes would meet his, like they had a long time ago, and they would tell him all he needed to know. She didn't notice him until he was nearly touching her. She lifted her head and turned, but not to face him. He saw her take the cardboard cup from the outstretched patched elbow of a tweed jacket. His ear began to throb, his arm ached and his foot hurt more than ever.

—◊—

20

'Ah! If it isn't the brawling barrister himself! Or should that be the mauling minister?'

The tweed sleeve stretched out towards him. The torn jacket responded.

'Good morning, my dear man. It's very nice to meet you again. Well, that is as long as you are not going to threaten me again.'

Cormac felt his cheeks redden.

'Yeah ... sorry about last night ... it was a misunderstanding. I don't make a habit of hitting strangers in pubs!'

'Oh nonsense, dear boy, to tell you the truth, it's the most excitement this old boy has had in years. Besides, after what this one's been telling me, we have something in common.'

He nodded towards Bernadette, whose eyes were flicking between his throbbing ear and his frayed jacket.

'You look like you have been at it again this morning!'

He tucked the loose flap into the gap Poppet had created.

'It's nothing really ... I was just rescuing a jogger and....' he thought of how the story ended. 'Never mind.'

She pointed to his ear.

'Your ear is pouring with blood. Here, let me see.'

She moved in close beside him, put her hand on his shoulder, and tilted his head. He hoped it would take her some time to find the cause of the bleeding.

'I think maybe you should go to the hospital.'

He knew he was not spending his day in Dublin in the Accident and Emergency Department of any hospital.

'Its fine, if you have a handkerchief or something, I'm sure it will stop in a minute. It doesn't hurt or anything.'

Peter passed him an initialled one from inside his jacket.

'There's a present for you. You can keep it if you promise not to hit me or run off with my wife!'

He laughed loudly at his own joke and Cormac knew they could never be friends. Peter turned to Bernadette.

'Well, my dear. Now that Romeo here has arrived, I shall be off. I bid you both a good day.'

He held Bernadette's arms, and kissed her on the cheek. He patted Cormac's back and strode purposely off the bridge in the direction from which Cormac had come.

He watched him leave. She was leaning over the bridge. Arms folded. Standing on one leg. Watching the flow of the river as it passed her by.

Cormac moved towards her. He leaned against the railings beside her. He was instantly annoyed with himself because it meant he couldn't look at her. Instead, they stood for a moment alone in their thoughts, side by side. He wasn't sure where to start. He hoped she would help him by saying something, anything. She didn't. She kept on staring into the gentle flow of the water. He felt the tension build inside him. The same tension he felt when he used to rise to his feet in front of a hushed courtroom. The fear he felt in the pit of his stomach and in the tremble in his legs when he rose in Parliament with hostile eyes fixed upon him from the benches across the chamber. No, she was in no mood to help him in any way. He was going to have to start. He did what he always did in the courtroom and in Parliament. He spread his legs slightly, fixed his knees against the metal in front of him, and focused on a point in the distance. He placed his hands firmly against the railings. The familiarity of the ritual released the knot in his stomach and steadied his legs.

'Thanks for coming, Bernadette.'

No reply.

'I didn't think you would.'

No reaction.

'I wouldn't have blamed you if you hadn't.'

Nothing!

He stepped away from the railings and walked slowly to the other side of the bridge. He leaned his back against the top of the barrier. He was looking directly at her back. She made no attempt to look for him. He felt he could have walked off the bridge and disappeared and she would have just remained where she was, fixed. Maybe he should walk away? Leave her there alone with her thoughts? No, he would wait for her. Wait until she was ready. He would stay with her, until she'd had enough of the flowing river and wanted to talk to him. In the meantime, he would simply stand still, look at her, and take simple pleasure in the fact he could.

One week ago, he had been locked in his study, frantically putting the finishing touches to the most important political speech of his life. It was undoubtedly the greatest speech he had ever written and he was sure it would be the greatest he would ever deliver. Apart from Annie, it was the only thing that mattered in his life, of that he had no doubt. It was a speech that would shape his long-term future and would cement his place as the heir apparent to the soon-to-retire party leader and prime minister. It would represent the final step in a twenty-year marathon of total commitment. No one at university had studied harder than him. No barrister in his chambers had researched more, taken on more cases, and won more lost causes. In Parliament, his stamina and stomach for a fight were legendary. Now, to his own astonishment, he realised he would sacrifice it all for a brief moment with her; his whole life for a stranger on a bridge he'd abandoned nearly a quarter of a century ago, when she was no more than a shy girl. He was still digesting the thought when she walked towards him.

'What are you doing here, Cormac?'

He was startled by the thin black tracks that ran down her cheeks. He was more stunned by the dark beauty of her eyes. He was hopelessly lost without his ritual. His stomach tightened, his legs took on a life of their own, and his mouth was devoid of all moisture.

'I just … I … just needed to see you … I … to say sorry … you know … sorry for what I did.'

'That's it, is it?'

Her tone was calm. Her posture suggested simmering anger. She walked back to her railings. He parked himself beside her.

She stared straight ahead and spoke to the Liffey.

'After twenty-two years and five months you needed to see me and say sorry! YOU TOOK YOUR FUCKING TIME ABOUT IT, DIDN'T YOU! I mean a week yes, a month maybe, a year at a push, but twenty-two years? FUCK OFF WITH THAT, CORMAC! Harry Crossan brought you into that bar last night. Up until the point when he spoke to me, you had no idea, and even less interest, in where I was in the world, let alone that I was in O'Donohue's. Harry is an interfering old fool who should never have brought you there … especially … and besides, I don't need you to say sorry, not anymore. I haven't needed you to say sorry for a very long time. You are nothing in my life but a distant and unpleasant memory and after this conversation today, I would be grateful if you could make yourself disappear again, thanks!'

Cormac was shaken. Her anger from last night had not only increased but had been joined by some new friends: hatred and disgust. He planted his feet and held the railings.

'Why did you come?'

No reply.

'If you feel like this, why did you come? You told me you weren't coming. You could have stayed away and you would never have to see me again. But you didn't. You came and that means something, surely?'

No response.

'Couldn't it mean you felt something when you saw me last night? I know I did.'

He felt a sharp sting on his arm where she had found the same spot as Poppet. The Liffey had lost its allure. Her black tracks had lost their moisture.

'Felt something! Jesus, Cormac! You really are something else. You conceited, self–centred, arrogant fucker! You think you can walk into the middle of my life and I will crumble into some girly wreck and profess my undying love for you? You arrogant prick - don't you think I fucked you out of my life ten boyfriends ago? You were gone by the time I finished my first year at university. What was he called again? Oh yeah, Paul, that was him, a psychology student. I thought I loved him as well, but then I realised his fumblings were not much better than your pathetic efforts. At least he was more reliable than you!'

—m—

21

They stood for a moment as the tension filled the silence. Cormac was unable to conjure up anything to say that might diffuse her anger. Everything he said last night and this morning only served to enrage her. He decided his best course of action was to say nothing at all. He would say nothing in the hope she might soften in the silence. He took in his surroundings. There was the vast and wild beauty of the Liffey, flowing gently beneath O' Connell Bridge. The Arlington Hotel stood proudly to his left, promising tourists traditional Irish dancing with their evening meal. An open-topped tourist bus sat outside it. He could just make out the driver serenading his captive audience.

'In Dublin's fair city
Where the girls are so pretty
I first set my eyes on sweet Molly Malone....'

He selected an elderly couple, waiting to board the next bus. American, he guessed, mainly due to the matching beige chinos. He watched them for a few minutes. They, too, stood in complete silence. But it was different. It was an easy silence, borne from a lifetime of love and laughter, trust and respect. They didn't need to talk. They were happy just to be. Each one secure in the knowledge that the other was there, had always been there, and would always be there. He watched them board the bus; disappear for a moment, before resurfacing on the top deck. He held her hand and guided her to the back seat. Cormac felt guilty as he watched the old lady kiss her husband's cheek. The bus moved off and he felt a sharp pang of envy. They were on their way into their day in Dublin. Just for a moment, he wished he could steal their day away. He kept them in view until they disappeared around the corner into O'Connell Street. He smiled as he heard their driver's first line.

'In Dublin's fair city....'

'What's so amusing, Cormac?'

His first impression was the silence had mellowed her. There was no aggression in her voice. It was just a simple question one person asks another when they discover that person grinning whilst staring into the space in the distance. Her shoulders were relaxed. Her head was tilted slightly to the right. She looked calm and elegant, apart from the parallel tracks that were now caked and flaking on her cheeks.

'Nothing, I was just miles away, watching the world go by. Hoping you would speak to me before I put my foot in my mouth again.'

No reply.

'Please Bernadette, even if it's only for this moment, and you never see me again, please just speak to me.'

'About what, Cormac? What do you have to say to me that will make any difference to my life, other than to make you feel better about yourself? I moved on from what happened a long time ago. I have no interest in going back there. Why would I and why should I? I have my life to live and you have yours. You have no part to play in my present or my future. You are just a boy who broke my heart a long time ago. I got over it and moved on and now I genuinely feel nothing for you; nothing at all.'

It was delivered with calm sincerity. He preferred her anger!

'Then why did you come, Bernadette?'

'For your mother.'

'My mother? My mother died last....'

'I know your mother died, Cormac. That's why I came. She was always very kind to me, and even after you left, I used to go and see her for a short time, up until I heard you had gotten married. She was a special person for me. She gave me the strength and the courage to move on and to help me to see that you were never coming back to either of us. So I came to say that I am sorry for your loss. I'm sorry that you cut her out of your life. I'm sorry that you missed out on her love, because she loved you with a great passion.'

'I couldn't come back, Bernadette. Not to her or to you. I don't expect you to understand that. Christ, I don't understand it myself anymore. I was told I could never see you again and I could never set foot in Ireland again.'

Her shoulders tightened again.

'Jesus, Cormac! It's not as if you were banished to Van Dieman's land or boarded a coffin ship to Ellis Island! You were only in Newcastle, for God's sake. You could have gotten a message to me. To let me know you were all right. You could have asked me to come to you. There was a time when I would have swum the Irish Sea and walked bare foot to you. Instead, for three years, I didn't even know where you were or what you were doing. Until one day your poor mother could take no more of my suffering and let me know you had moved on and gotten married. How fucking sick is that? I'm at her house every day waiting for news of you and you are off and fucking married!'

'I thought you said you were fucking your way through university?'

He hadn't even finished the sentence before he regretted saying it.

'I really had forgotten what a prick you can be, Cormac. Don't you dare try to second guess what I am saying to you. You do not deserve a conversation, let alone an explanation, of what I did to help me get over your cowardice.'

He put his hand on her arm. She moved as if he had shocked her with an electric prod.

'I am sorry, Bernadette. I had no right to say that. It's just ... it's like I am trying to find the right words but the wrong ones keep taking their place. Yes, I got married, and all I can say to you is that I was alone in the world and I knew I could never go back. Jill, she was a beautiful and kind person, and I needed her. I was grateful for her unconditional love and I desperately needed someone to love. I was terrified and lonely, desperately lonely. Don't you think if I could have, I would have sent for you? But I knew I couldn't. I knew I would be putting your life in danger. If anything had happened to you, I never would have forgiven myself. I sacrificed us, so you could have a life, so you could be safe. The only way they would let me live was if I gave up everything I loved: my country, my family and you.'

'What happened that night you left? I mean, I heard all the rumours that you were involved with the IRA and you were with Liam Conlon that night. I didn't want to believe them at first, but as time passed, it was pretty obvious, even to a naïve girl like me, that you were mixed up in it, Cormac. Did you do those things?'

He had always known this question would come, if he ever met her again, but still he wasn't prepared for it. He had buried the events of the night he left Ireland so deeply that not even Bernadette would be able to unearth them. It was as if they were the actions of another person. They were the actions of another person. He did what he promised himself he would never do to her. He lied to her.

'No, I wasn't mixed up with Liam that night. But he told me what was going to happen. I was threatening to go to the police about it. That's why they made me leave Ireland. Now if you don't mind, Bernadette, I would rather not go there again. It is very painful.'

He avoided her gaze. His palms were moist on the railings.

'Do you know what, Cormac? For the first time today, I really don't think I believe you. But it's no longer here nor there for me anyway. So you can lie, tell the truth, or do whatever you want to do. It's no longer my problem. I was just curious, that's all. But I will survive without knowing the truth. I still find it hard to believe that you would have been involved in something like that, but whatever.'

He smelt him before he heard him speak: sulphur and ammonia.

'Are you two ever going to feck off?'

Cormac was grateful for the rude interruption. He looked at the dirty little man who had arrived at his feet.

He was covered from his neck to his feet in a brown checked blanket. Cormac suspected it had begun life as a different shade entirely, but was reluctant to inspect it in any more detail. He held Bernadette's discarded cup in one hand and a card in the other, which read:

'DEAF AND MUTE. PLEASE GIVE GENEROUSLY!'

Cormac stepped back towards Bernadette.

'I am sorry?'

'Are you deaf, Mister? I said would you two ever mind fecking off?'

'I thought you were deaf?'

'Feck knows I wish I was! Having to listen to the shite you two have been talking. Now would you do a working man a favour and feck off this bridge? I have been working here for fifteen fecking years and I don't need a middle-aged Romeo and Juliet eating into me margins! Now, I don't mean to be rude, but would you both just feck off!

He felt Bernadette tug the back of Harry's jacket. When their eyes met, they smiled together for the first time in over two decades. As they walked off the bridge, Cormac looked back to see the deaf man check the contents of his cup.

He estimated that the fifty Euros would represent a significant boost to the talking mute's margins.

—⁓—

22

The weight of the holdall cut into his shoulder. He didn't mind the pain. He would have liked it to have been heavier, but The Chemist would be reasonable once he knew the significance of the operation. Once he appreciated the part he could play in the altering of the history of an entire nation, he would supply the necessary goods, even if he couldn't pay the full amount up front. What did something as insignificant as money matter at a time such as this? The Chemist would not let him down. They had a history together. They were comrades together in The Maze. Five years of torture together in that hell-hole made them practically brothers. Yes, they'd had a small disagreement but that was ancient history. The Chemist took over his role as 'officer commanding' in the prison, after he'd been prematurely relieved of his post. He wasn't happy about that. He felt The Chemist could have done more for him. Instead, he'd stepped into his role too quickly and with too much enthusiasm. But they'd sorted it like men. The Chemist came to his cell, and explained to him, face to face, that he'd no choice but to accept the position. It had been forced upon him from the very top. He explained he had no part to play in his expulsion from the movement. He promised one day he would help him recover his rightful place back in the fold. The thought made his jaw clench. They'd not only removed him from his post but expelled him from the movement. They said he'd used up all of his chances. Who the fuck did they think they were, humiliating him like that? He was a dedicated and obedient soldier who'd only ever served the cause to the best of his ability. Yes, he ran a tight ship inside. But the men responded to strong leadership and he was a leader. Everyone knew where they stood with him. Everyone knew the rules. Everyone accepted punishment would be swift and brutal when the rules were broken. How could they, those on the outside, those that knew nothing of life inside, possibly sit in judgement on him without even hearing his side of the story? How could they simply cut him off like that? Those same people who'd since led the movement down a cul-de-sac to oblivion and forsaken the armed struggle for a suit and a seat in Stormont. And expelled him for what? For delivering justice on behalf of a terrified boy who'd been violated by a notorious nonce? It wasn't pleasant and it was not as if he enjoyed it, but it was swift and brutal. The nonce was to be fed his own balls by the boy. When the boy couldn't complete his duty, someone had to. As O.C., the responsibility was obviously his. He'd read him the verdict. He'd made sure he understood the sentence and why he'd received it. The nonce fully understood and agreed with the punishment. He'd removed them with as much precision as is possible with a shard of broken glass. He'd held the old pervert's nose and waited for him to breathe. He'd forced one, then both down his throat and left him in his cell. With hindsight, leaving him to bleed to death was perhaps severe, but it was an error of judgement, nothing more. It didn't merit his total humiliation in front of his men.

The Chemist knew they were wrong to treat him with such disrespect. That's why he'd always made sure to keep him informed of any developments within the movement. It was The Chemist who'd stunned him with the news of the surrender. They had both agreed that their struggle wasn't over. They'd kept in touch in the years that followed and The Chemist supplied him with the little bits and pieces he'd required from time to time. He felt the old fella had become a too interested in the money on recent visits and less interested in the struggle, but on this occasion he would surely understand. This was bigger than any monetary reward. This was a chance to stand on the shoulders of giants!

He approached the GPO and decided his old comrade could wait a moment whilst he paid his respects to the men of 1916. He read the proclamation Pearse had so defiantly read on this very spot to a disinterested and angry nation; a nation preoccupied and fighting the wrong war on behalf of its very oppressors! But Pearse saw beyond the present. He hadn't expected the people to understand and immediately come to their senses. No, he knew he was sacrificing himself and his men for the greater good. He knew the British would do the rest of the job for him. They didn't disappoint him. In the days that followed, they'd executed him and ten others including Connolly, in a wheelchair; his wounds meant he couldn't stand to face the firing squad. The revulsion caused by the brutality of this response set in motion an irreversible chain of events and led to the expulsion of the British from twenty-six of the thirty-two counties of Ireland. He looked across the street to where Hobson must have stood frozen as he watched his former comrades give their lives for Ireland. Yes, he was to live longer in this world than they would. But they were now immortal! Yet they hadn't sacrificed themselves for twenty-six counties, had they? They hadn't died so future generations of Irishmen should live and die under British skies. No, they'd died so all Irishmen should be free! He flung the holdall over his other shoulder. He looked out across O'Connell Street. The words of Pearse slipped quietly from his mouth.

'The fools, the fools, the fools … they have left us our Fenian dead!'

He seeped into the morning shoppers and headed for Frederick Street.

'I have to go, Cormac.'

He'd barely limped off the bridge. She held her hand out like she was concluding a business deal. He felt a surge of blind panic. How could she want to go so soon? They'd only begun to break through the wall of her anger. He raised his hand to meet hers. He was not in such a quandary that he would miss this opportunity to touch her. He was not too proud, either.

'Please, Bernadette stay a little longer with me. Have a coffee, anything, but stay a while longer.'

She was already moving away from him. He held onto her hand.

'Why the great hurry?'

She loosened her hand from his grip.

'I told Peter I wouldn't be very long, and he's waiting for me at work.'

'Work?'

'Yes, Cormac, work! I have a lecture in ten minutes; or did you think that Dublin stopped working on the day of your arrival?'

He dragged his right foot as he tried to keep pace with her.

'Sorry, Bernadette, I just didn't think. I thought the beige suit was for me!'

She stopped.

'Well, you would, now, wouldn't you?'

He saw the second smile of the day.

'Anyway, what's wrong with the beige suit?'

'Nothing, you look beautiful in it. But then you would look lovely in that not-so-deaf bloke's blanket.'

'Piss off, Cormac. You always were full of bullshit. I suppose that's why you were always going to end up in politics!'

He felt his chest tighten at the thought she was aware of what was happening in his life after all this time. Had she been, after all these years, still seeking out snippets of information that would give away her true feelings?

'How do you know I'm in politics?'

She stepped towards him and took his hand.

'Could it be because I've never given up searching for you? Every day you have dominated my thoughts. Every waking moment, I've wondered where you were. Thought about who you were with. All this time, hoping and praying you would come back into my life.'

She dropped his hand.

'Or could it be my brother-in-law is Harry Crossan? Who even though you ignored him for twenty-two years, still thought, unlike me, the sun shone out of your absent arse, and therefore never shut up about you, despite the constant pleadings of those of us unfortunate enough to call him family.'

He reminded himself to thank Harry when he got back to the hotel.

'I think I've established which scenario is most likely, Bernadette. But you're here now, and we've not had a real opportunity to speak.'

She didn't reply.

He'd failed. She walked away. He couldn't bear to watch her go. He found a seat outside a window on the wall masquerading as a coffee shop and closed his eyes to block out the day. He heard the owner hurry to him.

'Will you still be around this afternoon?'

He opened his eyes and squinted at the silhouette in the sunshine.

'I was planning on being around for a while.'

'I only have two lectures today. So if you're around I'll meet you here after.'

He watched her as she walked away from him and vanished into the distance.

—⟋⟍—

23

He filled the first half hour by returning some of the forty calls he'd neglected. He called the prime minister, who'd left two messages, the second of which suggested he'd better have a very good reason for taking himself out of circulation. He'd always had a special bond with the PM, who'd been his very supportive pupil master when Cormac had been called to the Bar. He'd exercised extraordinary patience on the numerous occasions Cormac proved more a hindrance than a help. Although educated at Harrow and Oxford and hailing from an extremely privileged family, which had produced three prime ministers and two home secretaries, he was a man Cormac developed an instant bond with. He had the most selfless social conscience of anyone Cormac had ever met. He was unflappably at ease in any social gathering and had a genuine desire to better the lives and prospects of the most disadvantaged groups in the country. He was the politician and person Cormac aspired to be. He would often be kept awake into the small hours by the daunting prospect of following him into office. Cormac was proud of his mentor's achievements. He was looking forward to Friday's celebratory dinner at Hillsborough Castle, at which the PM was to be honoured for his part in brokering the peace in Northern Ireland that had finally ended the senseless bloodshed of the previous three decades. The Queen was presenting the prime minister with a Special Order of Merit in the presence of his four predecessors. Leaders from both sides of the community would be present, along with the taoiseach and members of the Irish Government. The PM invited Cormac personally, as a thank you for acting as his unofficial guide through the political minefield of 'The Irish Question.'

The phone had barely connected with a ring tone.

'Where the hell are you, Cormac?'

'Good morning, prime minister. Thank you very much for your kind words of condolence. The funeral passed off very well, thanks.'

'Oh, shit, Cormac. Please forgive my insensitivity. Of course, you poor man. I know how difficult it is to bury your dear mother. I lost my own a little over three years ago, and there's not a day when she doesn't enter my head. It is true what they say though about time and all that.'

'Thanks. I hope it is true, prime minister.'

'Without being rude, isn't it nearly a week since your mother passed away? I was under the impression you were anxious to get in and out rather sharpish?'

'I was, but circumstances changed and I thought I'd spend a couple of days here with Annie.'

'So will you be back in London to fly across to Hillsborough with the official party on Friday?'

To Cormac's astonishment, the thought of it filled him with dread, where only a week ago, not being on that flight would have felt like a catastrophe. He hadn't planned the words; they just developed a life of their own.

'I'll come back if you insist, prime minister. But if it is alright with you, would it be possible to spend the next couple of days here instead and report to Hillsborough on Friday night?'

'Yes, of course that's alright. I've been telling you to take a break for ten years. I'm only sorry it took the death of your dear mother to bring you to your bloody senses!'

He felt the now familiar guilt for his mother.

'It would be nice to spend a few days with Annie. You know, relax a little before she goes off to university.'

'Ah, Annie, yes. Spend a few days with her. What a lovely idea. What will you two be up to today then?'

Cormac squirmed. He hated lying; especially lying to the prime minister. But it was only a little one.

'We'll probably do a bit of shopping. Have a bit of lunch, you know, just watch the world go by.'

'Funny that, Cormac, I've had Jenny on the phone asking if I can get her a flight to Dublin and a ticket to a U2 concert. You wouldn't know anything about that, would you?'

He knew in an instant he'd been wrong to lie. How could he be so stupid? Annie spoke to the prime minister's daughter at least three times every day. More, now they were going to share a flat in Edinburgh for the next three years. He commenced his recovery.

'Oh, sorry, did I forget to mention we were in Dublin? Yes, I met an old friend at the funeral and came down on the spur of the moment. After she leaves me, after lunch, that is, Annie is actually going to the concert. Sorry about that.'

Cormac relaxed into his seat. *Good recovery.*

'So is Annie with you now, then?'

'No. She's taking her usual two hours to get ready.'

Too easy!

'So when Annie told Jenny she was on her way to Temple Bar with Claire and a lovely friend of her dad's called Harry, she was lying then, was she?'

He sat up in his seat. *Getting difficult!*

'No ... she's not ... lying as such ... what's happened there is she's forgotten ... she's just forgotten ... to mention I went out ... I couldn't sleep you see, so I went out early ... to you know, take in the sights of Dublin. I'm sitting here waiting for them, actually.'

Long pause. *Maybe, just got away with it?*

'Cormac?'

'Yes, prime minister?'

'What was my job?'

'What do you mean?'

'What was my job, indeed, our job, before we got into this godforsaken business?'

Definitely, absolutely, categorically, blown it!

'You were the most eminent criminal Queens Counsel of your generation, prime minister!'

Oh, fuck! Could you possibly be any more stupid?

'So you're off on a date with a mysterious woman from your past. You no longer wish to come back to England to fly with the official party on Friday. You've palmed your lovely daughter off on two relative strangers. And you are now lying to me, one of your oldest friends, and more importantly, may I add, the bloody prime minister! Have I just about covered it?'

No, you definitely could not have been more stupid!'

Harry's coat was suffocating Cormac. He removed it as best he could whilst remaining on the line. The back of his wet shirt was now uncomfortably cold against his seat. He leaned forward on the table to let the sun do its work.

'I am so sorr...'

'Cormac! Just shut up a moment. I have a meeting scheduled in two minutes. I only phoned because Jenny said you had a date and I was surprised and delighted for you. To tell you the truth, I was wondering if you wanted to bring her on Friday night. I know it might not be everyone's cup of tea, but there's enough novelty value to keep her entertained. Besides, I'm sick of losing my wife to you all night and having to listen to her tell me how much she wishes I was more like lovely Cormac O'Reilly. Lovely smile, lovely manners, and oh, that accent! That lovely accent! So what do you say? Do I get to meet the unlucky girl?'

He felt his stomach turn over. The thought he could actually bring her there overwhelmed him. To have her walk into that room, on his arm, as his partner, was more than he could ever hope for and more than he deserved. That was even if she wasn't already married and if she actually liked him! He thought it best not to lie again to the seasoned cross-examiner on the other end of the line.

'Thank you for the kind thoughts, prime minister. But I have two small problems there: she's married and she doesn't like me very much, I'm afraid.'

'I'm sorry about that, Cormac, but just a couple of observations from a wise old man. If she agreed to meet you, and has stayed for any length of time with you, forget whatever she says, she most definitely likes you. Another thing, if she is married and likes you, tread very carefully, young man, as better men than you have been brought to their knees by less. I suggest you take her for a stroll up O' Connell Street. At the top end, pause for a while at old Charles Stuart Parnell's statue, who in my opinion remains the greatest statesmen your little island has ever produced. He lost it all, Cormac, for his love of a married woman, for the love of his Kitty. See you Friday.'

24

During the prime minister's bit of fun at his expense, Cormac had drunk three cups of strong coffee provided by the surly Greek man who appeared, as if by magic, from behind the hole in the wall at regular intervals. Cormac suspected his host's mood was not helped by his refusal to purchase one of the dubious-looking cakes he was encouraged to partake of, on each of his visits to the table. Now he had another hour and a half to sit in a place he was not wanted with his head pounding and pulse racing from the overdose of caffeine he'd just been force fed.

He thought about strolling down the wide expanse of O' Connell Street to his left. He could glimpse the impressive bust of Daniel O'Connell, the Great Liberator, from where he was seated. The throbbing in his foot, which began the moment he rose from his seat, put paid to any thoughts of moving, no matter how distressing that would be for his tormentor, who was now vociferously shaking his head behind his little window.

He called Annie instead.

He called again. The noise on the other end of the phone caused him to swiftly remove the phone from his ear.

'Annie, can you hear me? Annie, it's Dad, can you hear me?'

She hung up. He was just about to ring again when her name flashed across his screen.

'Hi Dad, sorry about that - I couldn't hear a thing in there, it's absolutely jumping! Anyway, how's your date with Bernadette progressing? I'm guessing by the fact you're ringing me she hasn't exactly succumbed to the old O'Reilly charms? He looked at his watch. 11:30. *11:30 and Harry already has her in a pub!*

'It's not a date, and no, I think it's pretty safe to say she's fairly bullet-proofed as far as the O'Reilly charms go. Anyway, what are you doing in a pub at 11:30 in the morning?

He heard her loud sigh at his end of the line.

'Dad, sometimes I think you were never my age. I think you just popped out of the womb wearing a pinstriped suit, grey hair, and a frown! I'm in the pub because that's what people do on the day of a gig. You know, soak up the atmosphere, and build the tension with other excited people who want to do the same thing. Do you remember when you last went to a gig? Isn't that what you did?'

He tried to think of the last time he'd been to a gig. It came to him with a wince. It was U2 at Earls Court, maybe eight years ago. No, he hadn't been to the pub all day. He'd been in a very important and tediously boring cross party committee meeting, and begged a young Tory he didn't particularly know very well, or indeed like very much, to come with him, after his colleague let him down at the last minute. They didn't have time to get changed and so arrived at the concert suited, booted and very sober. His abiding memory of the event was having to explain to his new friend that the 'drunken yobs' who were jumping around and spilling their drinks everywhere were not, in fact, a menace to society but were behaving as they should at a rock concert. They left the gig early and instead spent the evening in a members club where they were joined by two more 'suits' and debated the inherent flaw at the heart of the government's recent economic policy. No, Cormac's last gig was not very rock and roll at all!

'Of course I remember what it's like going to gigs. I think 11:30 is a little early to be getting into the spirit of things that's all.'

'Oh, give your head a shake, you miserable oul' bastard!'

'Harry?'

'For Christ's sake, Cormac the wee girl is drinking orange juice and listening to some music. Would you ever listen to yourself? Do you not remember the time when you were sixteen and I'd to carry you to my house and clean the shit off you before you went home?'

Cormac cringed at the memory.

'Is Annie still beside you, Harry?'

'Yes, she's right here.'

'Oh, well, cheers for the old, 'your father shit himself' story there, partner! She couldn't have lived without that one, I'm sure!'

'I'm just pointing out the hypocrisy of parenthood, my friend. We're all guilty of it. Listen, she's a sensible girl and I'm here with her until about six o'clock, so no harm will come to her. When you're finished with Bernadette, if she hasn't finished with you already that is, what say we rendezvous at the hotel, or are you intending to blow me out for the whole trip?'

In truth, he wanted to stay with Bernadette for the whole trip, and if in the unlikely event she agreed, then he categorically would 'blow out' Harry and Annie and anybody else, for that matter.

'Absolutely Harry. I'll meet you at six and thanks for looking after Annie for me. Could you put her back on, please?'

'You're forgetting something, my friend.'

'What's that?'

'You owe us an apology for being a prematurely middle-aged boring bastard!'

He had a point.

'I'm sorry, Harry.'

'Hang on one moment, my friend. That's better now. What are you sorry for again? Say it loud, Cormac.'

He looked to the window. His tormentor was not there. He said it.

'I'm sorry for being a prematurely middle-aged boring bastard.'

'Louder!'

'I'm sorry for being a prematurely middle-aged boring bastard!'

'Louder, like you mean it, my friend!'

'I'M SORRY FOR BEING A PREMATURELY MIDDLE-AGED BORING BASTARD!'

He heard a crowd cheer on the other end of the line to match anything U2 would receive at Croke Park that evening, and then they hung up.

He glanced at the window and to his relief, the grumpy waiter was nowhere in sight. He relaxed into his chair and giggled at how he could be so gullible and at his old friend's relentless juvenile stupidity.

'Would you like me to call you a doctor or get you some help, sir?'

He turned and smiled weakly at the frowning man with coffee and cakes standing over his right shoulder.

—⚬—

25

By the time Bernadette returned, he'd spent a very pleasant hour eating delicious cakes with his new friend, who wasn't Greek but Romanian. He'd travelled alone to Dublin two years ago to find work. He was six months away from being able to send for his wife and five children, whom he hadn't seen since the day he left. From the many photographs, Cormac concurred that Nicolai junior most definitely had his father's strong jaw line and little Nadia was indeed in outright possession of the most beautiful smile in all of Romania! Cormac agreed there was no need for him to visit Romania to verify this matter as it was clearly already settled!

He was still looking at the photos when the chair beside him scraped across the stone.

'What a beautiful little girl.'

He lifted his head from the photograph.

'Oh, Bernadette, I'm sorry - I was in a world of my own.'

She was sitting as close as one could be to another without any part of their anatomy coming into contact.

'That's quite alright, they are beautiful children.'

He looked at her. Her black tracks were erased and replaced with a touch of foundation. Her eyes, while large and bright, were, however, sat on two puffy shelves that told him instantly that she'd spent a considerable portion of their brief time apart in a less than happy state.

He leaned into her.

'I'm sorry I was distracted because it meant I missed the opportunity of seeing you walk towards me.'

Her seat scratched the ground again so there was enough space for another person to fit between them - two, if they were small.

'Cut all that crap out, please, Cormac! We're not love's young dream anymore! Can we just establish from the off that I came back to spend the day with you for old time's sake as much as anything, but that is it. When today is done, it is done, and we can both move on with our lives.'

He pulled his chair into the space.

'I'm sorry, Bernadette. I shouldn't have said that. It comes out involuntarily. Thank you for coming back and I'm very grateful we can spend this time together. I can't help noticing though, you have been crying. I hope I've not caused that?'

She shook her head and searched the sky.

'There you go again! How many times, Cormac? No, you didn't cause this. You stopped causing this a long time ago. My best friend from work left today, that's all, nothing more, OK?'

'OK.'

She ate two cakes and ignored Nicolai's valiant attempts at selling Cormac's many virtues.

'Well, Cormac, you're the tourist here, so what sights would you like to see in Dublin today?'

He resisted the urge to say 'you and only you,' and instead asked her what she would recommend. She reeled off more information than he suspected the Dublin tourist board possessed. He considered his many options but one overrode all the others. He pointed across the bridge.

'Can we ride on the top deck of one of those?'

She spat her coffee, narrowly missing Nadia's smile.

'You want to ride on the tourist bus and be fed all the blarney?'

He thought of the old couple this morning.

'Yes, that's definitely what I'd like to do.'

They thanked Nicolai and headed for the bus.

Maybe he could steal their day after all.

He hauled the bulging holdall up the last flight of stairs. It had taken him an hour to reach the hotel. It was a journey that would ordinarily be completed in fifteen comfortable minutes. He'd been forced to set it down every few paces along his short route from The Chemist's hostel on Fredrick Street to the hotel on Lower Dorset Street. He pushed it through the door and flung himself on top of the single bed. Things hadn't gone according to plan, but when he looked at the contents of the holdall, he felt satisfied with his day's work. He had everything he needed and more. The Chemist proudly showed him how both devices would work and he was more than satisfied with the goods on offer. The fucking price, though? He was shocked when The Chemist named his price. He shouldn't have been, because lately the old man had been getting greedy. He was very calm at first, and thought they would haggle for a little while, and then the old man would take what he had to offer. He was five grand short. How the fuck was he supposed to find that amount of money in this tiny window of opportunity? He told the greedy bastard not to fuck with him, not now, of all times! Not when he stood on the threshold of immortality! How could the silly cunt possibly think he could present him with the perfect tools and then take them away like that? What was he supposed to do when faced with that? Say 'thanks for the demonstration; I'm sorry I can't quite afford them today, maybe some other time?' Didn't the greedy old fucker know there was no way he was leaving without the goods? He tried everything with him. He warned him not to make him angry. Not now when there was so much at stake.

He told the old man he didn't want to fall out with him. He liked him, for fuck's sake! He begged him to let him have the goods and he'd never trouble him again. He even told him he would make sure the rest of the money would be there before the end of next week. He informed him of his duty to provide what he needed. He must do it, not for himself, not for the money, but for Ireland! It was then he knew. He knew as soon as the old fucker said Ireland didn't pay his bills. He knew the old man was not a true patriot. He was like so many others he'd met in the movement. He was a phoney; a fraud; the enemy.

It was surprisingly easy. Once he saw the old cunt for what he was, he felt the rage overtake him. He'd seen it at the door on the way into the dingy little room. The sun was glinting off its shaft. He made up his mind in an instant. He relished the moment to come. He enjoyed telling the greedy cunt he was leaving. He savoured the slow walk to the door, feeling for the grip of the club behind the coat that partially obscured it. He spun in an instant and caught the old cunt above his left ear. He'd helpfully walked right onto the perfect spot. The shaft bent slightly as it swished its arc through the air before it hit his head with an exhilaratingly loud crack. The collision of club and head sent a shudder right to his shoulder. The cracked head followed the rest of his body in slow motion to the floor. The greedy old fucker was looking up at him, begging him to finish it. On the sixth swing, he was sure the job was done. It was not like the others. There was no crack. There was no resistance. It was like sliding into fudge.

He cleaned himself up in the stinking bathroom. He worried for a moment about someone finding the body. He was concerned this might complicate things a little. Then he remembered the old man complaining he was the only other person he'd seen in months. No, it would not be a complication. In two days' time, this would be an irrelevance. He closed the door gently on the traitor with a golf club in his brain and made his way here with the goods, the money, and the contents of his cabinet.

His bandaged hand was pounding from the jarring of the golf club. His shoulder ached from the weight of the holdall. He felt desperately tired from the afternoon's exertions and tried to close his eyes to sleep. It was useless - the adrenaline from the kill was still raging through him. He sat up, rummaged through the bag, opened the contents of The Chemist's cabinet and poured two thin parallel lines onto the bedside table. He paused for a short while, deciding whether or not to 'hoover' the table. He knew the safe thing to do was to stay in the room until his transport arrived in the morning. He stared at the holdall on the floor next to the door and contemplated his day's work. The lines on the table meant he would not be in control of his evening and would never stay in his room after having them. He thought about Cormac and Annie enjoying their day in Dublin. Friday would be a big day for all of them - if they were having fun, why couldn't he?

He bent his head to the table.

—⁓—

26

He reached the top deck and headed for an empty seat near the back. He squeezed himself in as far as he could to make plenty of room for her. She slid in to the seat in front of him and half turned to face him. He quickly got over his disappointment when he realised that at least he had a good excuse to look at her. The last time they shared a bus together she fell asleep on his shoulder on the way home from a day trip to Portrush. He could still recall the smell of apples from her hair. He woke her to complain that his arm had gone to sleep. He made her move away from him until the feeling had tingled its way back. Today he was sure that if she wanted to sleep on his arm for the next week, he would most definitely let her, but for now, he would settle for her presence and the fact he could look at her. The bus idled for ten minutes while the driver encouraged tourists to join him on his magical mystery tour of Dublin. The seats all around them filled one by one in rapid succession. To his relief, the bus finally pulled from the stop with their seats intact. The driver was commencing the first line of 'Molly Malone' when the two middle-aged, perfectly groomed women emerged into the light of the top deck. They walked past two blindingly obvious spare seats and parked themselves next to him and Bernadette. For the next thirty minutes, he talked to the back of her head. The disinfected woman on his right strained to listen to his every word whilst appearing to be engrossed in the colourful brochure on her lap that she hadn't bothered to open. On the driver's second rendition of 'Molly Malone', he admitted defeat in his quest to steal the old Americans' day. He leaned into the back of her head.

'Let's get off at the next stop.'

She twisted as far as she could, considering she was being jammed against the side of the bus by the equally nosey neighbour to her right.

'What's at the next stop?'

He scanned his brochure to establish were they were headed but before he could make any sense of it, he was helpfully informed by his nosey lady that Kilmainham Gaol was the next stop.

She spoke as they joined an official tour along a dimly lit corridor of Dublin's latest tourist attraction.

'You sure know how to show a girl a good time, Cormac!'

'Stick with me, girl, there's plenty more where this came from!'

He smiled at the triviality of her remark and his response. Even as a shy teenager, she always made him feel completely at ease in her company. He never had to try hard or to worry about saying or doing the wrong thing. They just simply connected on their first date, and slipped into a rhythm only they could understand. He recalled his mother's conversations in the kitchen, which acted as futile warnings they were too young to be getting so serious with each other. They paid no attention. It was always them against the world. They promised each other it would always stay that way. It should have stayed that way, but he shattered it; shattered her. He squirmed at the memory of the promises he made to her. All of which he broke. He was fortunate she ever agreed to speak to him again, let alone spend the day with him.

'Bernadette.'

'What?'

They made their way into the central atrium of the prison.

'Thanks for today. I know it is more than I deserve. I let you down more than any other person in the world and that is unforgivable. You of all people! The person I....'

She put her finger to his lips.

'Please, Cormac. It's all ancient history. Let's just enjoy our day together. I am not really interested in going back there. I ... we've both come a long way since then. Too far to ever go back. I don't know about you, but I'm starving and I'd really like to get out of this prison if that's all right with you.'

After another ten-minute ride on the bus, they were seated by the window of a little ethnic café she insisted they visit, in a side street off Grafton Street. Cormac scanned the menu, which was all hummus, couscous, and vegetable tagines. His appetite had already left him by the time the dreadlocked forty-something waitress arrived at the table.

'Hi Bernie, I haven't seen you in ages.'

Probably been no protest marches in ages.

'No, I've been really busy with work and my writing. How have you been keeping?'

She pulled up a chair next to Bernadette.

'I'm keeping the very best and John has been on at me for ages to organise something for you. You know, before....'

Bernadette cut across her.

'Sorry, Sheena, this is an old friend of mine, Cormac O' Reilly. He's only here for the day and I thought he couldn't visit Dublin without sampling the best cooking the city has to offer.'

If you're a lesbian, vegetarian, serial political protester!

'I'm sorry Cormac, I was so busy gassing there I forgot my manners. I'm Sheena McGoldrick, part-time chef, part-time actress, and part-time wife when there's a handsome young man such as you in my restaurant! Or has this dark-haired temptress already snared you?'

He felt uncomfortable with the sentiment. He looked for guidance from Bernadette, who was also looking uneasy with where the conversation had gone.

'Sheena McGoldrick, you old floozy, leave the man alone, can't you see he is embarrassed? Anyway, I'll tell your John on you if you don't hurry up and take our orders!'

Sheena sighed theatrically and stood up at the table.

'What a shame, Cormac. I was thinking if I could get you into a jacket that fits, a hair cut from this century, and knock a few pounds off, you could have taken me nicely into my old age. Ah well ... *c'est la vie*, my young lover, *c'est la vie*!'

She removed the back of her hand from her forehead, winked at him, and produced a pencil from the depths of her blonde dreadlocks.

'Now, what's your pleasure Cormac?'

Without much enthusiasm he settled for some hummus and warm pitta bread followed by a vegetable tagine and couscous, all washed down with a carrot and orange juice.

When did Bernadette get into this stuff? What is so wrong with a nice red and a fillet steak?

Sheena wrote it down with a quizzical frown and turned to Bernadette.

'Usual, Bernie?'

'That'll be great, and could we have some extra chips with that?'

Chips! They do chips! They can be discreetly placed in the pittas to make posh chip butties! That's something, at least!

'What are you thinking, Cormac?'

About making chip butties with your chips and my pittas, actually!

'Oh ... nothing really - just what a nice little place this is and how friendly Sheena is, that sort of thing.'

She leaned back in her chair.

'Some things in life still amaze me, Cormac.'

'Oh? What's that, then?'

'Cormac O'Reilly the vegetarian! I'd never have thought that, not in a million years!'

He leaned forward and pointed an accusing finger.

'I'm not a vegetarian! You're the one who brought me here!'

'Yeah ... they do the best lamb curry in all of Ireland and I had a recollection of you dragging me to some Indian restaurant on the Lisburn road once a fortnight for a whole year!'

She turned his menu over so he could see the full range of meat, poultry, and fish dishes Sheena had to offer.

'So you're not a vegetarian?'

'No, I'm not a vegetarian, Cormac. Anything else?'

'Are you a serial protestor?'

'No, though I've been to the occasional one when I was at university, but mainly for the free alcohol afterwards! Next question?'

'Have you ever....? No, it doesn't matter!'

She leaned across the table so her hands were nearly touching his.

'No Cormac, I've never been a lesbian either! And I can't believe you are still doing that after all these years.'

'Doing what?'

'Making sweeping judgements about people based on a two-second glimpse of their lives.'

'It usually works quite well.'

'No, Cormac, it doesn't work well at all! You only think it does because you never get to find out what the people are actually all about, or who the hell they are, you never stop to actually ask them. You assume that your stupid stereotyping is correct and they are what you think they are!'

He was enjoying her mock consternation. She was in full flow.

'Take Sheena, for instance. Tell me what you think of Sheena?'

He let her have it.

'Second marriage, no kids, smokes a bit of dope, likes the odd protest, has at least two tattoos, has had at least one nervous breakdown, been to Jamaica once, and currently has a boyfriend as well as her husband!'

She laughed so loudly she brought the staff out of the kitchen.

'Jesus, Cormac! You really are some piece of work! Sheena, up until last year, was the foremost neurosurgeon in Dublin. She's been married to John, also a surgeon, for eighteen years. They have three children, one of whom has severe disabilities, which is why Sheena gave up her post and now only works in this, her sister's restaurant, one day a week. As far as I'm aware, she has no tattoos, doesn't smoke dope, and has never had a boyfriend or a breakdown, in all the time she has been married. She has, I'll grant you, been to Jamaica on more than one occasion, so I suppose I should say well done for that one, Sherlock! What do you have to say about that?'

'See? I told you she had been to Jamaica!'

The napkin hit him on the face as Sheena emerged from the kitchen with several enormous plates of food. Bernadette insisted they share the lamb curry. She helped him with his tagine, which to his surprise was as delicious as the curry. Sheena sat with them for a little too long over a glass of red wine. When she'd gone, and they were readying to leave, Bernadette spoke.

'I came to look for you once.'

He sat back down on the chair.

'When?'

She looked like she wished she'd never said it.

'Oh, I don't know. It was about six years after you left. I convinced some unsuspecting girlfriends Newcastle was the centre of the universe for nightlife. They didn't take much persuading and we went for three days. I heard you were a barrister, so it wasn't difficult to find you at the courthouse. I checked three different courts before I found the one you were in. I sat in the public gallery, two feet away from you. You looked so different - maybe it was the wig, but you looked so grown up. You never looked up from scribbling and sat behind a really pompous, deep-voiced midget, who liked the sound of his own voice so much he nearly put me to sleep. My heart was nearly bursting through my chest. Six years and I hadn't even had a boyfriend. I never did quite sleep my way through university. I sat outside the courthouse to wait for you. I plucked up the courage to speak to you, even though I had been told I was never to contact you again. In my head, you were still my Cormac. I waited for an hour, and then you finally came out, walking behind the midget with the deep voice. I started to walk towards you as quickly as my wobbly legs would take me. Then they came around the corner. The little girl got to you first. She was so excited to see you. Then the woman followed. She was tall with dark hair and impossibly long legs. You kissed her and smiled and before I could move, you walked around the corner and disappeared from me again. That was the point, Cormac. That was the point when I had to let you go. I know you let me go a long time before that, but I just couldn't do it until then. I walked along the quayside as a stranger in the city you'd made your home and I could hardly see where I was going. I was blinded by grief. Grief for what I had lost. For what I could never have again. Now I can sit here with you right in front of me and it feels normal. I feel nothing. It feels right that we can be with each other for this brief moment in time and I can just let it pass. That we can meet as old friends and simply move on.'

He removed his gaze from the pepper pot and studied her face. There were no tears, no emotions telling their own tale in her eyes. She moved on a long time ago. How long had she held on? Six years? She waited for him for six years! What kind of a love was that? What kind of devotion? What kind of a love was that to lose? The thought unsettled the food in his stomach.

'I am sorry, Bernadette. I never knew. I wish, now more than anything, you'd spoken to me. I wish I had possessed your courage, but I was a coward then and I'm a coward now; a frightened little boy who never quite learned to grow up. For what it's worth, the girl with the long legs was my nanny for six years. She used to pick Annie up for me and bring her to meet me at the end of the court day.'

The clock behind her head told him it was 5:45.

'I'm meeting Harry at the hotel in fifteen minutes, but I'm not ready to leave you yet.'

She paid Sheena and kissed her on the cheek.

'Peter is not expecting me just yet, so if you don't mind waiting here for ten minutes with Sheena, I'll pop across, get the car and give you a lift. I wouldn't mind a wee chat with my brother-in-law. Besides, you'll never make it in ten minutes with that limp.'

She looked at Sheena.

'Will you look after this one for a wee minute while I go and get my car?'

Sheena took his arm and winked at Bernadette.

'Take as long as you like, love. I'll look after *him* alright!'

He missed her the moment she closed the door.

—⚬—

27

Bernadette's knowledge of Dublin was significantly superior to Harry's and they arrived at the Burlington with minutes to spare. The hotel car park was bulging and she let him out at the front door whilst she drove out to the street to leave the car.

His foot was feeling a little better as he hobbled to where he was certain he would find his friend. The disinterested John Travolta look-a-like behind the bar told him to look next door. No customers had been in the bar since the commencement of the wedding reception. He shuffled across the marble hall and glimpsed Harry propping up the bar. He appeared to be engaged in a heated conversation with the father of the bride or groom. The band at the far end of the crowded room was performing a very impressive rendition of 'The First Cut is the Deepest.'

As he approached the door of the banqueting hall, Harry was up off his seat and dragging him urgently across to the round man in the uncomfortable looking penguin suit.

'Here's the very man to settle this one, Dermot!'

Cormac looked at Dermot, whose cheeks looked like they were still storing the wedding banquet he'd just eaten on behalf of the rest of the guests. His angry red snout suggested the pint of Guinness he swigged and placed on the bar in order to extend his hand to Cormac would clearly not be his last of the day. Harry was tugging at his jacket.

'Cormac, I've a very important question to ask you. Now think very carefully before you answer, my friend, there's a lot at stake here.'

The glazed look in Harry's eyes revealed he hadn't been partaking of orange juice along with Annie this morning, certainly not without the addition of a vodka or two in it.

'What's at stake, Harry? And what time did you leave the girls at? I thought you were staying with them until six o'clock.'

Harry eventually steadied himself on his stool and positioned his elbow on the bar, just in case.

'There's a hundred Euros at stake and I left the girls at two. Sorry, that is not correct; they left me at two. I was beginning to cramp their style with the young suitors that were gathering, know what I mean?'

Harry's elbow momentarily slipped off the bar. He recovered well by bouncing his shoulder off the brass rail and returning to some form of equilibrium. Cormac suppressed the rising fear that always gripped him at the thought of Annie becoming a woman and instead concentrated on ending Harry's dispute with Dermot. Dermot, by this time, was in possession of another half-drunk pint of Guinness and a thick creamy moustache, which filled the entire space between his thin lips and fat nose. To say he was unsteady on his feet would not be technically correct. His feet, as far as Cormac could ascertain, remained the only thing solid in his entire body. He was in perpetual motion! So much so that Cormac found himself preparing to catch his bulky frame on at least three occasions, for fear he would land on the tiny grey-haired woman who stood behind him nursing a large tumbler of whiskey. She looked so familiar that Cormac found himself scanning the room on the off chance Poppet was about to finish the job she started so well this morning!

'Harry, what's the question?'

'What?'

'The question … you know … the important question that had you two at each other's throats when I came in?'

'Ah the question … yes … the question is….'

He looked at Cormac and then at Dermot.

'The question, my friend, is this….'

He froze as if someone had pressed the pause button.

'Harry, what was the fucking question that was so important ten minutes ago?'

His eyes were closed, as if he'd just been switched off.

Cormac turned to Dermot, who at first appeared like he'd shrunk during the course of the conversation. He realised he'd merely widened his stance to give himself a bit more purchase on the floor. It had worked to some degree, as the little woman with the foul mouth and comparable temper was no longer under any immediate threat.

'Don't suppose you know the question, Dermot?'

'What?'

'You don't happen to know the question you were arguing with my friend about?'

'What question would that be, then?'

'The ques… Oh it doesn't matter… can I get you a drink there, Dermot?'

'That's very kind of you, *Conor*, I'll have a wee pint of Guinness with you, but that's all, mind you, I don't want to be too drunk before me speech. The daughter has me warned to be on me best behaviour!'

'Harry Crossan, would you look at the bloody state of you?'

She had just found the on switch. Harry sat up in his stool and balanced perfectly without the assistance of his left elbow or the bar.

'Bernadette, I didn't think you'd be coming back. I thought....'

'Ah, give over Harry! And come and give me a hug. I didn't get a proper one off you last night.'

They embraced warmly as he lifted her from the floor. Cormac turned his head away to shield himself from the easy familiarity of their ritual. His two oldest friends, whom he now barely knew, whose relationship had grown and blossomed into an unbreakable affection for each other, while he merely skirted around the edge of them both.

'What's happening with you and our Roisin, Harry? I haven't heard from either of you for months and I can't get hold of her on any of the numbers I have. I came by to see if you could enlighten me or maybe give me her new number, and then I'll be off.'

Harry glanced down at him.

'Could you give us a minute, Cormac?'

They were both staring at him, still locked in their embrace.

'Yes, of course, forgive me. I'll be in the bar. Come and get me when you're finished.'

He made his way across the busy reception area. What the hell was he thinking, standing there like a nosey neighbour gawping at them? They were family. They had important private things to talk about; things that he would never be part of; things that he'd chosen not to be part of.

He spent the next hour alone in the bar, except for the occasional grunt from John Travolta or smile from the Polish girl, who, to his increasing dismay, was working yet another shift. He occupied the time by trying to guess each song played by the wedding band, who were quite clearly caught in a time warp beginning in nineteen sixty-three and ending in nineteen seventy-nine. Harry would have been most impressed with him, as he was sure he correctly guessed all but one. Some seventies one-hit wonder.

> *'I wanna kiss you all over*
> *Over again*
> *I wanna kiss you all over*
> *Till the night closes in....'*

He nearly got it as the chorus continued.

> *'Stay with me, lay with me*
> *Holding me, loving me*
> *Ba...a...aby.'*

No, it was definitely gone. But he knew a man who would take great pleasure in telling him who it was. Indeed, who the lead singer was, who wrote it, and what he had for breakfast on the day in question!

He'd just volunteered 'Dorothy Moore' and 'Misty Blue' to the extremely underwhelmed barman when Harry and Bernadette approached the bar. Her eyes had rediscovered this morning's puffiness and Harry had found his balancing ability again. Cormac spoke as they reached him.

'Would you like....?'

She didn't let him finish.

'I have to go, Cormac. Thanks for today. Bye.'

She was already on the turn. The swiftness of her words and movements rooted him mute to the stool. He knew she was going. He knew he didn't want her to. He also knew he was powerless to stop her.

Harry spoke for him.

'Dance with him, Bernadette.'

She rocked to a halt.

'What?'

'You heard me. In the circumstances, there would be no harm in dancing with him.'

She glanced at Cormac, whose legs had found the courage his mouth hadn't. He walked towards her and took her hand.

'Please, Bernadette - for old times?'

She shook her head and placed her arms so lightly on his shoulders he could barely feel them. They swayed gently together as Dorothy's whole world turned misty blue and then halfway through the song, something changed in her. It was only slight, barely noticeable at first, but for a moment, he felt her move into him. Her grip tightened and she held on like she would never let go.

Then it was over.

Before the song finished she was off and running towards the hotel exit. He stood for a second in numb silence and then limped after her as fast as his foot would let him. By the time he had reached the pavement, she'd vanished. *How could she just run away from him like that? Now, of all times, when he felt her connection again. He would not let her go like this. He would ask Harry to take him to her. He knew she had Peter now, and if she told him that is where she wanted to be, then he would let her go. But not like this.*

'She's gone, my friend.'

Harry sat on the wall beside him.

'You know where she lives, Harry. Take me to her, please. I only want to speak to her, just for a minute. I can't just let her run off like that.'

Harry put his arm around his shoulder.

'I am afraid I can't do that, my friend.'

Cormac turned to face him.

'Surely you know where your own sister-in-law lives?'

The big man stood and talked to the evening sky.

'Oh Cormac, I'm so sorry. I'm sorry I brought you here. I never should've interfered. I should've left the past where it belonged.'

Cormac looked up at his huge frame.

'No Harry, you're wrong. It was the best thing you have ever done for me or could ever have done for me. I can still feel it, you see and I think for a fleeting moment back there, she felt it too!'

The big man turned and crouched beside him.

'Oh, Cormac ... you just don't get it, do you? She's gone, and she's never coming back, my friend. I don't know where she lives. They moved three months ago, in preparation for emigrating to America. They're leaving in the morning.'

It felt like Harry had punched him, with all his might, full in the stomach. He started to get up and realised his lead-filled legs wouldn't let him.

'Emigrating? Why didn't you tell me they were emigrating? Why didn't she tell me?'

'I can't speak for her, my friend, but I only found out twenty minutes ago. She was going to leave when you were in the bar, but I told her it wouldn't be right. That's why I told her to dance with you. Now let's get inside. I don't know about you, but I could do with a drink.'

They walked past the spot were she'd stood and held him as they danced. The same place he thought she was holding on to him was in fact where she was letting him go. Harry ordered the drinks and Cormac thought of Pat Molloy from Tallaght all those years ago. Had he, like old Pat, merely danced with another man's wife at the Burlington? He found a weary smile. *Yes, Pat, Bernadette was definitely worth the beating!*

—⚬—

28

He arrived back at the hotel at midnight. He staggered into the dirty little bar for a nightcap. He was frustrated and angry. The thrill of the events at The Chemist's hostel and the effects of his last hit had now completely left him. He ordered a double vodka and looked around the room. An old school Dublin alcoholic stood in his familiar stupor at the end of the bar talking to an invisible friend. In a dimly lit alcove behind him sat a teenage junkie whore, with a greasy, well-dressed man who could have been her latest client, but judging by her scab ridden face, sticky hair and filthy grey tracksuit, was more likely her disappointed pimp. Not a U2 T-shirt in sight. No sign outside declaring the pub the Official Headquarters of U2 for the day. He used to like U2 a long time ago. Cormac was always more keen than him and Harry. What did Harry like again? Fucking Simple Minds - how appropriate for that gormless big cunt! He listened to U2 in the car with Cormac the night he'd been betrayed by him. The last night he spent with his old friend. On the way to the house, Cormac put the album on for him to listen to. They drove on their first operation together listening to the beginning of 'Where the Streets Have No Name.' Cormac kept rewinding it over and over again until they reached the house. There was no sign the cowardly bastard was going to ruin him at that point. Yeah, that put him off U2 all right. That and the constant spouting of Bono about things he knew fuck all about. He was already serving fifteen years in the Maze for doing his bit for Irish freedom when that cunt was in America pontificating about how sick he was of Irish Americans coming up to him and talking about the revolution back home. What had he said on stage? Oh yeah, 'fuck the revolution.' A fucking sound bite from a pop star preacher, who lived in his ivory tower in Dublin and fuck knows where else! Had he ever seen his father dragged out of his bed and beaten by the butt of a rifle in front of his screaming wife and kids? What the fuck did that pretentious cunt know about growing up in Killane or Belfast or Derry during the troubles? Fuck all, that's what! He'd never been arrested for simply walking down the street and humiliated at Castlereagh for three days and nights.

He ordered another drink and bought one for the old alky in the corner. Yeah, better here than in the city centre. He knew if he'd stayed, he would have drawn attention to himself by fucking over the couple of U2 T-shirt wearing pricks who were starting to take the piss out of him. He considered for a moment taking them out the back of the pub and biting the faces off both of them. Any other day he would have really enjoyed that. That would teach them to fuck with him. No - he was proud he was able to leave before the rage came and spoiled his night completely. He was still angry when he got to the door of the hotel, but now he was calm.

He ordered a night cap and allowed himself to think about tomorrow. He could taste the terror Cormac would feel when he realised the choice he was faced with. He ached for the moment when Cormac O'Reilly MP realised Liam Conlon had outsmarted him, caught up with him, and now owned him! He thought of Friday night, watching the news break, the scampering reporters, all fighting for the best vantage point; all scratching their heads at the simple brilliance of the mastermind behind the biggest terrorist attack on the establishment since 9/11. He was on the threshold of shaking the established order to its foundations. He knew there was little chance of sleep tonight.

He shook the pimp's hand.

He started out low.

He'd have happily paid double for her.

—◊—

29

By the time Cormac reached the car park, Harry had already started the engine. Annie and Claire were curled around each other in the back, desperately trying to make up for the sleep they'd lost last night. He'd been delayed in trying to find the young Polish girl who lived to work in the hotel. He found her, looking completely exhausted, sweeping tables in the deserted bar. She appeared very grateful for his words of advice on her 'work-life balance' and her mood was further elevated by the two hundred Euros he gave her. His lowered somewhat when she said it was only fair that she share it with her twin, who worked the evening shift last night while she was at the U2 concert and Lily's Bordello until four o'clock in the morning!

He was convinced he'd gotten less sleep than the girls, though he was pretty sure by the look of them the quality of their experience outweighed his considerably. He gave up trying at four-thirty when his head threatened to explode with his constant replaying of the events of the day with Bernadette. The signs were there. She refused to talk about her marriage or future plans. He tried to talk about Annie, to no avail, and she showed no real interest in his life or his future. She was not someone who was ever intending to stick around and move forward with him. He was annoyed with himself for being so stupid.

They hardly even knew each other. If he was brutally honest with himself, only a week ago, she would've barely registered in his thoughts at all. Yes, all that happened was he'd let a bit of silly nostalgia get in the way of reality. He'd allowed his grief to unhinge him for a short while. It was as simple as that. If that was the case, and he was sure it was, then why did he feel like his heart had been ripped from his chest, stamped on from a great height and shoved back in the wrong way?

They eventually reached the outskirts of Dublin, forty minutes after they left the hotel. Harry managed to drive around in circles for the first thirty and only admitted he was lost when an old traveller tapped the window and asked him if he was looking for anyone in particular on the fifth occasion they'd driven onto her site next to the docks.

Cormac was grateful the girls were asleep after their constant, and he suspected, still drunken, details of the concert. Harry was in no mood to talk and he suspected that was mainly due to his three-hour stint with the bride's father at the wedding. His phone buzzed silently in his trouser pocket for the fourth time in ten minutes. He looked at the missed calls. He didn't recognise the number. All four calls were from the same number. He listened to the latest message.

'Hello, Cormac, it's Maggie here. The thing is ... the thing is, Cormac ... I was wondering what you and Annie were doing this afternoon. You see Jack and me would like it if you could call for some lunch, or just a cup of tea ... he hasn't got to see you and well I would like to a ... you know ... I would like to a... apologise for my behaviour the other day and I.... I don't want Annie

... or you, in fact, going back to England on that note ... so if you could give me a call back on this number which is 0777... 0777... Oh I can't remember... but Jack says it will come up on your phone... God bless.'

'Trouble?'

'What?'

'The message you just listened to. By the look on your miserable face, I'd say that was trouble!'

He sighed and placed the phone back in his pocket.

'Not trouble really - it's just Maggie. She wants us to call for lunch or something.'

Harry opened a toffee to satisfy his sugar craving.

'What's the problem? Why don't you go for an hour and tell her I've organised something back at my place and you can't disappoint me. She is your big sister, Cormac - it wouldn't cost you very much to cut her a bit of slack and spend an hour of your time with her, would it?'

Cormac unwrapped one of the toffees Harry hadn't offered him.

'It's just I was thinking of going home tonight and travelling back with the official party tomorrow.'

'I thought you'd cleared it with the prime minister you'd make your own way there.'

He removed the toffee which was hurting his tooth.

'I did, but I'm not really that comfortable about hanging around Killane, if I'm being honest.'

Harry unwrapped another toffee.

'Don't, then. We'll call at my place; you get the car, see Maggie for an hour, and come back and hide out with your old mate who incidentally you have ignored for the vast majority of this trip. Besides, Annie and Claire are having a great time and they can go out on Friday night while you're hobnobbing at the castle.'

He looked at Annie snoring in the back seat, all arms and legs with Claire and realised he'd taken her to Dublin for two days and spent hardly any time with her. He would take her to Maggie's and then spend a day with her wandering around Hillsborough, just the two of them. He was painfully aware that those times he'd taken for granted, all these years, were coming to an end. He looked at the signpost, which told him they'd crossed the border. He agreed with Harry. What possible harm could come from spending one more day in Ireland?

—∿—

30

The quick shower at Harry's propelled Annie into overdrive again. Cormac felt a surge of relief when Maggie's cottage surfaced on the horizon. This was tempered by the dread he felt at the prospect of the uncomfortable hour ahead. Tom's revelations of Maggie's lost child stirred strong feelings of guilt in him that nevertheless failed to override his lifelong dislike of her, and everything she stood for. He bent to tie his lace at the edge of the footpath. This allowed Annie to experience the full awkwardness of the initial hug and gave him an early indication of which way Maggie would lean for his ordeal. One wrong guess later and they were into the small but perfectly decorated living room. It smelled of his mother and of lavender. Maggie busied herself in the kitchen and returned with a tray and three china cups. She was out and back again in a fussy instant, with a brand new teapot and a small mountain of chocolate biscuits.

'I'm sorry Jack is not back yet, but he won't be long, I'm sure.'

She noisily carried the cup and saucer to Annie. Seeing them together, they could easily be mistaken for sisters. He shuddered at the thought.

'So, Annie, how was Dublin?'

Cormac braced himself for another twenty minutes of 'the stage was amazing,' 'the Edge's guitar was like a one-man orchestra,' 'Bono' this, 'fluorescent jacket' that. He picked up a biscuit and sat back to suffer in his silence.

'It was brilliant, auntie Maggie, and Dad met up with Bernadette, his old girlfriend, didn't you, Dad?'

He coughed out the biscuit that lodged in his throat. Maggie swiped it into a napkin and lost all interest in Annie.

'You saw Bernadette in Dublin?'

He tried to volley the conversation back to his grinning daughter.

'Yes, I bumped into her in the pub. Annie, why don't you tell Maggie all about the concert? I'm sure she'd love to hear what a great night you and Claire had.'

She didn't rise to the bait. He persevered.

'Annie got on really well with Harry's daughter, didn't you, love, and Claire is even thinking of trying to change her university and go to Edinburgh, isn't that right, love?'

Maggie poured herself some tea and sat on the settee beside him.

'Ah, what a lovely girl Bernadette is. What a crying shame you broke her heart like that.'

She pointed a chocolate finger at him and spoke to Annie.

'Did he ever tell you how he broke that young girl's heart Annie? Oh, sure it nearly broke his poor mother's heart, lord rest her. That wee girl coming to the house, all those years, just so she could get a wee bit of information about what this one was up to.'

He felt an urgent need to defend himself before the jury retired to consider its verdict.

'Oh, Maggie, come on now, it happened a long time ago. It's all in the distant past. Bernadette told me she used to go round to see mum once a week for a little while after I left. I'm truly sorry for what I did, but life goes on.'

The chocolate finger was waving close to the end of his nose but her eyes were on Annie.

'Would you listen to this fella. Jesus Christ, God forgive me for swearing, but that girl never missed a Saturday with Mammy for nearly seventeen years, which is more than can be said for him! Even after she married that lanky fella from Dublin, she still came to see Mammy once or twice a month. Sure wasn't she here only last Saturday, and going on and on about how she was so excited that she'd seen her Cormac on some late night political rubbish during the week.'

Her voice seemed to fade into the distance as the pounding in his head competed with the thumping in his chest. He rounded on her.

'You're lying. Why would you do that? Why would you lie about something like that?'

He slumped back in the chair and knew the answer before it came.

'I beg your pardon. I don't tell lies, Cormac. It's the God's honest truth. She was here on Saturday with Mammy. She wanted to take her out in the car but she wasn't feeling very well. Mammy loved her and she used to sing for her. Mammy loved to hear her sing. She sang for her in the living room on Saturday evening with only me and Mammy for an audience. What is it they call that song she used to sing specially for her?'

She started to hum it gently. He recognised it in an instant. He felt his throat close.

'It's 'Bright Blue Rose', Maggie.'

'That's it. How'd you get that so quickly?'

He closed his eyes to hide the pain.

'Because she was still singing it for her the night we met.'

His phone rang loudly and he was glad of the excuse to leave the room. He glanced at the number and it didn't register as someone he knew. He wouldn't ordinarily have answered it. He stood up and walked to the kitchen.

'I'm sorry, I really must take this call.'

He closed the door on Maggie and Annie and on his embarrassment and his shame.

He didn't recognise the frantic voice on the line.

'Cormac, please don't say anything, especially to Maggie, but it's Jack here and I desperately need to speak to you.'

He'd never had a conversation with Jack and knew little about him apart from he was Maggie's husband and he didn't approve of Cormac's chosen career.

'Obviously it is difficult to do that right now, but I'll obviously try to help in any way I can.'

The phone was silent for a moment.

'I'm at the graveyard. I wouldn't ask normally but I'm desperate and can't face Maggie with this. I'm begging you; please could I just have a moment of your time before I speak with her?'

He was sure he could detect fear in his voice.

'I'll help if I can, but can't you just tell me on the phone?'

'Cormac please, I can't come home until I've spoken to you in person, it just wouldn't be right. It'll only take ten minutes of your time. Please do it for Maggie, if not for me. Please hurry.'

The phone died.

He paused for a moment to gather his thoughts. He had no particular desire to speak with Jack or indeed help him. But he'd said he couldn't come home until he'd spoken with him and the graveyard was only five minutes away. What would he tell Maggie and Annie? Maggie opened the kitchen door.

'Is it safe to come in yet, you're not discussing state secrets or anything?'

She'd given him his opportunity.

'Actually, Maggie, that was a rather important call; I'm afraid I'm going to have to pop out for a little while, but I'll be back shortly. Will you look after Annie for me?'

He could tell she wanted to reprimand him. Tell him how typical it was of him to put his career before all else. She poured more water into her teapot and settled for theatrically rolling her eyes.

'If you must, but don't be too long. Jack will be here in a minute.'

He had little difficulty explaining to Annie, who'd endured a lifetime of let downs when, as an ambitious young MP he'd be held up on one occasion and have to dash off on another. As the front door closed behind him, he was grateful for the few minutes it would take to drive to the graveyard. It would allow him to digest Maggie's revelations. He was still trying to make sense of it all by the time he pulled into the deserted graveyard. There was no sign of Jack or anybody else, for that matter. He'd said he was at the graveyard, hadn't he? Cormac was already reversing his car when the silver Mercedes pulled up on his right hand side. Jack climbed out and walked around to the passenger side of Cormac's hire car. He waved an apologetic sorry at Cormac before he opened the front passenger door, and slid in. It struck Cormac, he'd taken so little interest in his family over the years, he hardly recognised the fair-haired, mouse-like features of his own brother-in-law. As Jack got into the car, Cormac promised himself in future he would make more of an effort with Maggie and with him. He would invite them to visit, maybe for a weekend on the first occasion just in case; but a weekend was the least he should do. This was his only sister and her husband, after all. Her husband, who was obviously in distress, judging by the moisture streaming down his forehead as he turned to Cormac.

'Jesus, Jack, are you all right?'

Jack's tiny red eyes flicked between Cormac and the rear of the car.

'I'm sorry, Cormac.'

'Sorry for wha....?'

Both rear doors opened and shut in an instant. He felt the cold steel of the muzzle on the back of his neck and in his bowels. He glanced at Jack, who was already making his way out of the car. The owner of the revolver spoke with a broad Belfast accent.

'This is the situation, Minister. You're now the property of the True Irish Republican Army. It's my orders to escort you to a meeting with our Commanding Officer. I'm also instructed to shoot you, if at any point, I feel you're not compliant or present a risk to myself or my fellow officer. Do you understand, Minister?'

Cormac meant to say, yes he understood, and yes, he would comply.

'The True Irish Republican Army? You must be fucking joking?'

The blow to his left temple sent his head crashing against the door window and quickly focussed his attention.

'Do you understand, Minister?'

He rubbed his temple to check for blood.

'Fully.'

'Now slowly move to the passenger seat.'

The back door behind the driver's seat opened and closed, and a skinny, spotty teenager slipped behind the steering wheel. The youthfulness of the driver gave Cormac a false sense of courage. How naïve were these people to let him see their faces? Surely they were nothing more than stupid kids? His next thought was not so comforting. How naïve was he, a government minister gallivanting around Killane with no security and no thoughts for his or his family's safety? If they were naïve, what did that make him? He was the one sitting in a graveyard in Killane with a gun at his head and an underage fanatic about to drive him to God knows where. The driver started the engine and reversed out past Jack, who was sitting with his head bowed behind the wheel of the Mercedes. Cormac's nervousness would not allow him to remain silent.

'Aren't you going to blindfold me or something?'

The voice with the gun sniggered.

'I don't think that will be necessary in the circumstances, but if you don't mind, could you pass me your phone, thanks.'

They turned left out of the graveyard and headed back the way he'd come. Cormac's thoughts turned to Annie. What would happen to Annie if he were never to return? How would her life turn out? The thought he might not be there for her made him shiver uncontrollably. He talked to the gun in his neck.

'Where are you taking me?'

He got an instant reply.

'Home, Minister, we are taking you home!'

—⁓—

31

They drove past Maggie's house and he thought he saw Annie at the window. For a moment, he thought about throwing himself out of the car as it travelled past the house. Maybe they'd drive on and leave him there on the road with nothing more than a few bruises. Annie and Maggie would hear the commotion and come out to tend to his minor wounds. He could get inside and make one call and they would be arrested before he'd been to casualty to have his minor cuts and bruises seen to. He and Annie would be on a plane out of Aldergrove before nightfall. The cold steel jammed into his neck ensured the thought passed as quickly as it had entered his head. He watched old Fr. Mackie close the door of the chapel behind him as he went to bring God to the congregation who'd stopped bringing themselves to God. The car slowed as it approached his childhood home. The gun jammed into his neck as the boy's heavy foot hit the brakes.

'Listen very carefully, Minister. My comrade will get out of the vehicle and when he gives you a signal, you'll walk casually up the front path as if you are just home from work for your tea. I'll be walking two paces behind you and if you so much as take a step out of time, I'll happily blow a hole in you, before heading back up the road to pay your wee daughter a visit. Do you understand?'

Cormac said nothing. He was too caught up in thoughts of Annie. No matter what happened to him, he had to make sure she was alright. She would be alright! She'd realise something was wrong when he didn't come home and she'd call someone, or do something. She was a bright girl. She'd know what to do. Now was not a time to die a hero. That would achieve nothing. He felt a sharp pain in his ear.

'For fuck's sake, do you understand?'

His head cleared.

'Yes, I understand.'

He followed the spotty boy along the garden path, concentrating on his worn Adidas trainers. Cormac was sure had seen better days, probably when their first owner had worn them out five years previously.

Cormac walked through the front door of the house he'd left behind forever only three days before. It felt more alien to him today than it had when he had entered it in the dead of night, after a twenty-two year absence, earlier in the week. Something had changed. Something was fundamentally different. As he entered the living room, he realised what that difference was. It was the smell. His mother's house always had the same smell. He couldn't tell what that smell was, but he'd recognised it, even the other night, while she lay cold in this little front room. He'd smelled it in Maggie's earlier today. He wondered if it must be the O'Reilly scent. If other families have that unique smell only they would recognise. The smell was now gone and was instead replaced by a pungent, masculine smell, like a changing room at a gym that has been left full of used clothing and has not been aired for a week. The voice with the gun, who now possessed a face as spotty as his friend with the second-hand trainers, pushed him down onto his mother's settee. The room was exactly as he'd left it, except his father's kitchen table sat where his mother's coffin stood four days ago. There was only one kitchen chair positioned on the other side of the table from where Cormac was seated and now accompanied on either side by the acne brigade of the unit. It looked like the work of someone who wanted to feel important.

'Is your big boss not around boys?'

The spotty boy, without the gun, answered.

'He'll be here in a minute.'

'Where is he?'

The spotty boy, with the gun, answered.

'Fuck up! It's none of your business!'

'What's he doing?'

Spotty Gun-less answered.

'He's in the toilet having a shite, if you must know. He's always in the toilet, isn't he, Patrick?'

Spotty Gun spoke across him to Spotty Gun-less.

'You fuck up as well dopey, and it's just as well it doesn't matter that this fucker knows my name, otherwise I would have blown your knees off two seconds ago, Ciaran.'

Neither Spotty spoke again. He heard the upstairs toilet flush.

It was no surprise to Cormac when he strode through the door. It was still a shock to see him. As the years passed, Cormac began to allow himself the indulgence that he would never again cross paths with him. In the early days after he left Ireland, he was tormented with the fear that this day would eventually come. On more than one occasion, Cormac was convinced he'd seen him lurking in the shadows. He would look up to search for him, but he was always gone again. He'd been the cause of endless nights of torment, both in his nightmares and the terror-filled darkness that followed them. In recent years, the nightmares ceased, but he never completely got over the sensation that he was always a presence in his life. He'd just learned to live with the gentle uneasiness those feelings caused him. They were the background hum to his daily existence. No, it was no surprise to see him stride past his head and position himself behind the kitchen table. It was most definitely still a shock.

He retained the handsome features that made him the envy of the boys and the subject of nudges from the girls at school. He was tall, with thick, jet-black hair, now greying a little at the edges. He possessed high cheekbones that any aspiring young model would pay money to replicate. His eyes were a shade of blue so vivid they looked unnatural, as if he'd placed blue lenses in them, or dyed them for effect. His only flaw as a boy had been the explosion of teenage acne which left its still-visible mark on his now slightly fuller jowls. Three things struck Cormac as he sat facing him. He looked like he occupied a world without colour. His clothes were predominantly black. Black boots, black jeans, black shirt, grey T-shirt, and long black leather trench coat - not exactly classic summer mood-lifting shades. His grey pallor indicated a lifetime of careless living and his skin glistened with a thin film that he wore like a mask. By far the most striking feature of his appearance was his eyes. They were the same deep blue colour, but they were changed completely. They had once been his most attractive feature, but now appeared to be vibrating in their sockets, as if at any moment, they'd burst out of their uncomfortable, tormented prison. At this point, they were fixed firmly on Cormac. The silence sent the first trickle slowly down the inside of Cormac's shirt.

He stood up and strolled around the kitchen table and perched himself directly above Cormac's head. He clasped his hands tightly in front of him, as if he didn't trust them to hang loosely by his side. He smelled of chemicals and poor hygiene. The trickle that was becoming a river forced Cormac to speak.

'Hello, Liam.'

—◊—

32

His jaw tightening was the only response.

'Do you mind telling me what I am doing here?'

He unclasped his hands and sat on them.

The river was developing into a gentle torrent.

'Look, Liam, I....'

'You always did talk too much, comrade.'

He moved his hands onto his lap and clasped them again.

'I'm not your comrade, Liam. I'm a British Government minister and I'd like to know why you brought me here.'

He leaned forward so Cormac could add alcohol to his list of smells.

'I fucking know what you are. I also know what you were, comrade.'

Cormac tried to hide his growing anxiety.

'Liam, you've obviously brought me here for a purpose. Now, if you don't mind, could you explain that purpose to me, or are you going to sit there and try and scare me for the rest of the day?'

He laughed without his features responding. And spoke as if Cormac was still in nappies.

'Ah ... there now, is the little comrade scared? Is he going to run away again? Going to promise to be a good little boy from now on and tell tales on that naughty Liam?'

They acne brigade giggled in unison.

'Liam, I don't know....'

'ENOUGH!'

He bent into Cormac's face like he intended to take a bite. He paused for a moment so Cormac could experience the full terrifying effect. By the time he retreated from the pose, Cormac was forced to wipe his forehead to prevent the salty water from stinging his eyes.

He removed his coat and moved behind the desk to signal the pantomime was over and today's business was about to begin.

'Here's the deal Cormac. At five minutes past eight tomorrow night, I'm going to kill your daughter. That's my starting point in today's negotiations. Now I'm sure you'll be delighted and relieved to know that, like all negotiations, I can be persuaded to adjust my terms accordingly. Now I presume you would not want that to happen, and if that is the case, the first thing I need you to do for me is to ring wee Annie and tell her to go with Maggie and Jack for a couple of days and you'll pick her up on Saturday morning.'

'Why would I tell her to go with Maggie?'

'Maggie has kindly agreed to look after her for me until it's time.'

'Maggie is working with you?'

'Great old couple, Maggie and Jack. Obedient servants to the cause, and not too fond of you from what she tells me.'

Cormac rubbed his hands across his wet face. *Liam was going to kill Annie and Maggie was going to help him?* It was too ridiculous to bear consideration.

'I don't believe you.'

'Look Cormac, let me enlighten you a little. Help you understand. Make it easier for you.'

He rocked back on his chair.

'I like wee Annie. I always have. Well, when I say always, I mean since I started taking an interest in her life. I think she was about fourteen then. Over these past few years, I've felt like a father figure to her, or a guardian angel, if you like. Though some of the thoughts I've had about that wee girl over the years, maybe father figure is not the right term, if you know what I mean?'

Cormac swallowed to stem the rising nausea.

'Now, after looking out for her all these years, the last thing I want to do is to kill her. I've seen her develop into a beautiful young woman with the whole world at her fingertips. I even helped along the way. What was the name of that flash young fella who had the accident with his knees? Ah … never mind, but you can see I've no real interest in harming her. So if you'd like to take the first step to ensuring she has a future, you'll give her a ring and tell her to stay with Maggie and Jack. Oh, by the way, give Happy Harry a call too and tell him you've changed your plans for this evening.'

Cormac was dismayed at how easily Annie was appeased. Harry was more difficult to lie to, but eventually backed down and wished him good luck for the evening. Liam took the phone off him and removed the gun from the spotty boy's tired grip.

'At this point, comrade, you're free to come and go as you please, but understand if you choose to leave before we have reached an agreement, you're passing an immediate death sentence on your daughter. At the moment, she's scheduled to die at five past eight tomorrow night, unless you and I come to an alternative arrangement.'

Cormac put all thoughts of Maggie's betrayal to the back of his mind, now a crowded place jammed full of regrets at his own stupidity which had landed him here with this unhinged madman.

'Tell me what I have to do to save her.'

Liam leaned forward and placed his elbows on the table.

'You have to be brave and do your duty for Ireland. Now, I know only too well, both those things don't come easily for you. That's why I had to involve poor innocent Annie as my insurance policy, in case you decided to run away from your responsibilities again.'

Cormac ignored the remark.

'What do you want me to do?'

Liam opened a holdall that was positioned just between his legs. He pulled out a black Samsung mobile phone and set it carefully on the table in front of him.

'I want you to bring this with you to Hillsborough Castle tomorrow night. If you do that and you have it with you at the official function in the banqueting suite at eight, when I call you, then at five past eight, Annie will be released from custody and free to take up her offer of a place in Edinburgh. If at any point from this moment and until then, you fail to comply, she will die!

Cormac studied the chunky little object on the table.

'I don't understand. When you call me, what do you want me to do?'

Liam laughed and the puppets on either side of Cormac joined in. He walked around the table and leaned into Cormac's face, so he could inhale his stale breath. He spoke in a barely audible whisper.

'Die for Ireland, comrade. Like you swore you would all those years ago. I want you to die for Ireland alongside the British scum that have persecuted my people for far too long. I want you to die and kill them all alongside you; every last one of the established order in that room.'

He casually walked back around the table, rocked the chair back, stretched and yawned. He brought the chair gracefully onto all four legs again and smiled at Cormac.

'So there you have it, comrade. There's your choice in black and white.

You die or Annie dies! Not a great choice, I'll grant you, but a choice nonetheless. It's certainly better than what you had at the start of this negotiation, but probably not what you were ultimately hoping for, but, as you know, that's the nature of negotiations. So what's it going to be then, comrade?

You or Annie?'

—⚭—

33

Cormac ran the cold tap, cupped his hands and felt nothing when the water hit his face. He looked in the mirror and didn't recognise the frightened shadow glaring back at him. He tried to take a deep breath to slow his racing heart but his lungs refused to suck the air in. He sat on the closed toilet lid and desperately tried to calm the constant ringing in his head. He lifted the lid quickly as his bowels reminded him they were still as fragile as ever and were now operating in overdrive. He felt a sour rush in his throat and vomited on the bathroom floor in front of him, disabled as he was by his pressing need to remain exactly where he was. On countless occasions of great stress, both in court and in Parliament, he feared the very public embarrassment his bowels might cause him, but never, until today, had they ever let him down on this scale. Liam only finished his sentence when they reacted in an instant and Cormac sprinted in vain for the tiny little bathroom at the top of the stairs. His face, arms and legs were now streaked in a cold sweat that oozed out of every pore and dripped onto the floor alongside the contents of his stomach. This was the third time he'd been forced back on the toilet since he scrambled here, in his blind panic, forty minutes ago. His soiled underpants lay, as a mark of his shame, in the bath where he once played as an innocent child.

He stared at them and he knew the time had come.
He was finally going to pay for the sins of his past.

An hour had passed by the time Cormac felt able to leave
the bathroom. He entered the darkness of the living
room. The room always darkened early in the evening
due to the inadequacy of the window design. It was the
result of an architectural error made during the council's
mass production of these tiny terraces, to accommodate
the ever-increasing overspill from West Belfast, in the
late fifties and early sixties. His father would forever
complain he couldn't even read the afternoon paper in
his own living room on a summer's day. He'd invariably
be forced, grunting and cursing, into the brightness of
the narrow kitchen, for a nightly row with his mother, as
she flitted in and around him, setting places for their
evening meal. How he'd love to turn the old clock on the
mantelpiece back. He'd give anything to experience just
one more day of his childhood, listening to them pretend
to argue vehemently, whilst all the while, their obvious
love for each other remaining never far from the surface.
The darkness of the room never made any sense to him
as a child. He couldn't understand how the sun could be
lighting up the sky and this little box would need a light
on by midday, even in the middle of July. As he sat on
the settee and watched Liam playing with a laptop at the
kitchen table, the room now made perfect sense. The
darkness was waiting for Liam to make it complete.

He didn't lift his head from the screen to acknowledge
him as he slumped onto the battered leather settee.
Cormac, in order to quieten his bowels, tried to imagine
the events of last Saturday in this little space. He tried to
conjure the sound of Bernadette's voice, singing to his

mother and visualise their relaxed conversation, borne of years of familiarity. The image of his mother in an open casket and Liam's presence, made him swiftly abandon his hopeless efforts. He felt his stomach gurgle and his pores release their first droplets.

Liam closed the lid and turned his attention to Cormac.

'I've ordered you a sausage supper from the chippy, or do you no longer do that sort of thing? Is it more canapés and caviar these days?'

His eyes were momentarily at peace, but the thin sheen of moisture was still very evident, even in the darkness of the living room.

'I don't want anything to eat, thanks, and yes, I still do that sort of thing. I still do it a bit too often.'

Cormac started to pat his belly, but stopped when he recognised the pointlessness of it. This was not an occasion for the self-deprecating banter he always fell into as an ice-breaker in any number of social settings.

'You really should eat. We can call it the last sausage supper!'

Liam laughed at his own gallows humour. He came around the table and sat next to Cormac on the side where Spotty Gun-less had vacated, presumably to drive his comrade to the chip shop for tea. Cormac found himself worrying for the state of their complexions before Liam buried the triviality of the thought.

'So what's it gonna be then, now you've had time to think it over?'

Cormac clenched every muscle from below his ribs to his legs to fight his bowels' natural reaction to the question.

'What's the point, Liam?'

'What do you mean, what's the point?'

Liam was lying back on the settee next to him, like he'd called to pick up his old friend for a night out on the town. Cormac felt able to relax his abdominal muscles a little.

'What point is served by the mindless murder of the Queen, four prime ministers and all the other people in that room from God knows where?'

Liam didn't move anything except his eyes, which turned to meet Cormac's gaze.

'I'd have thought to an intelligent chap like you it'd be pretty obvious. Look at the world around you. September 11th, what was the point in that? It caused revulsion all over the world, didn't it?'

He sat forward as though he recognised this was not a point that should be delivered from a slouch.

'Look what else it did, though. It produced, and still is producing a brutal response from the West. Which in turn, and here is the simple beauty of it, ensured a fertile breeding ground for so-called terrorist groups to grow and prosper. Every time a child dies at American hands in Afghanistan or Iraq, another grief-stricken mother, father, or brother, joins the fight. Do you suppose they think about the pointlessness of September 11th when they enrol? No, of course they don't. They were probably as horrified as you were when they watched the first plane hit. No, they're responding to the brutal response from the West. They only see the dead girl, murdered by an American bomb that landed on her school, or on the market place while she was there buying a birthday present for her mother.'

He rose from the chair and began pacing the length of the short living room.

'So when you say it is mindless murder, then I suppose you are right. It is the response I am after that makes it worthwhile. This country has been seduced by the gloved fist of Britain on too many occasions to mention; never more so than today. Who'd ever have thought an Ireland that remains divided and chained to Britain would ever be so passive and submissive about it? When we signed up to the armed struggle, it was with one objective in mind: to unite this island and have her stand among nations as a free nation after eight hundred years of occupation and doffing our caps to John Bull. We've been sold out. The people have been seduced by the political establishment; by fine words and a promise of a tomorrow that may never come. You ask what the purpose of tomorrow night is. Tomorrow will change the course of history, don't you see? There'll be revulsion at first. There'll be pleas from all sides that we should never go back to the 'troubles,' but most of all, history has shown, there'll be a brutal response from the British. The wolf will reveal itself again and the people will see the true relationship between these islands once more. It'll be revealed for what it always was, and always will be, until we drive them out; one of master and servant. Pearse and Connelly were reviled for the Rising. The whole country was disgusted by this rabble, who dared to challenge the British while their sons and daughters were fighting in Flanders for the empire. After the executions, though, everything changed; once the glove came off and the fist smashed down again, then the people awakened from their slumbers and there was a new beginning. It's a response to the response I'm after. History has shown the inevitability of both!'

He sat back down on the settee, utterly convinced by his own warped logic. He looked at Cormac through eyes that were vibrating against their sockets again. Cormac focussed on a point above the clock.

'You're very wrong, Liam. The people have moved on. They've had enough of suffering. They want to live together, side by side, and build a future for their children, free from the hatred and suffering they've endured. The people will not respond in the way you think. The British Government will not respond in the way you think. You'll only strengthen the resolve of all parties to push on with the process. It's no longer reversible, Liam. This is not nineteen sixteen and you're not Padraig Pearse. You'll be committing murder for murder's sake. At least call it as it is, instead of sugar coating it with some mixed up, out of date thinking, which renders you nothing more than a dinosaur. You're a relic and you're sick, that is all. This is not about your love for your country. This is not about your fight for freedom. This is about your sick lust for blood. You were unstable all those years ago and you're unstable now. If you lived in any other country in the world, you'd simply find another cause to hide behind. Something else to fight for, to give you the thrill you get from killing. How many members do you have in your True IRA Liam - four? five? ten? If you're lucky? I've never even heard of you, nobody has. Nobody has heard of you, because you exist only in your own head and maybe in the heads of impressionable children like the two you sent out to fetch your dinner. You want me to carry a bomb into Hillsborough Castle tomorrow night so you can kill fifty innocent people? If I don't do it, you'll kill my daughter? Why don't you just accept it, Liam, you want *me* dead? If you accept that point, then maybe we can move forward from here. Give me your gun and I'll shoot myself in the head and you can watch. I know how much you would like that, wouldn't you? I'll do it for your pleasure, but then you must let my daughter live. You said this was a negotiation, well they are the only terms that are acceptable to me.'

When he finished, he looked at Liam. He was dialling a number.

'Hello, this is OC Liam Conlon calling, can you hear me clearly? I want you to find the nearest convenient ditch from where you are. I want you to pull the car over and I want you to shoot the prisoner in the face and leave her in the ditch by the roadside. Before you shoot her, I want you to call me, so I may play the events to my audience. Do I make myself clear?'

He hung up. Cormac searched his face. Only one conclusion could be reached. He was not bluffing. The phone rang. Liam answered.

'Are you in position?'

He didn't pause, or look to Cormac, or give any indication he was about to retract his orders.

'You may....'

'STOP! Stop, please! I'm begging you! Stop! Please don't hurt Annie! Please! I'll do anything you want, but don't harm her ... don't....'

No more words could find their way through the convulsions now tearing through his entire being. He was crying like a baby who suddenly realised its mother had escaped from its watchful eye. The contents of his nose were mingling with salty water and gathering as a paste on the edges of his lips. His hands were not there to wipe it away. They were occupied in trying to tear his hair from his head. He pulled himself to his feet and turned to face Liam. He had the phone resting on his lap.

'Is she alright?'

'Do we have an agreement?'

'Is Annie alright?'

'Depends on our agreement.'

Cormac looked at the phone and at Liam's eyes and sat back down on the settee, defeated.

'Yes, we have an agreement.'

Liam put the phone to his ear.

'Ignore that order. Continue as previously planned. Await further instruction.'

Cormac slowly felt the fog clear.

'Thank you.'

'Not at all comrade, it's me who should be thanking you. Tomorrow you are going to make the ultimate sacrifice for your country. Just one thing to remember, so there's no further confusion; it's my absolute understanding that we have reached an agreement suitable to both parties. As of this point, the terms are strictly non-negotiable. Is that clear?'

Cormac didn't respond.

'Is that clear?'

'We have an agreement and the terms are non-negotiable.'

—⟋⟍—

34

Cormac poured himself a glass of water and sat in the table-less kitchen. The room appeared twice its normal size now the OC of the TIRA commandeered the table as his status symbol, like some Nazi general who'd recently taken up residence in the best house in the small French town they now controlled. He scanned the mobile phone that Liam had happily returned to him once they agreed terms. There were six missed calls and two messages. The second was from Annie.

'Hi Dad, just calling to see how you're keeping. I'm just on my way with Maggie and Jack. I was going to call at Harry's for a change of clothes until I realised you had them in your car. Never mind, Maggie says I can borrow some of hers. Oh, Maggie sends her regards and says not to worry, she'll look after me for you. Don't work too hard; you're supposed to be on compassionate leave. Love you.'

He tried to call back, but it was dead.

The other message was from his constituency agent to remind him of his up and coming summer fair responsibilities in Northumberland the following Saturday. Liam had left the black Samsung on the kitchen table in the living room and told him he was free to do whatever he wanted between now and eight o clock tomorrow evening. His first thought was to get out of the house as quickly as possible, contact the prime minister and explain everything. He'd know what to do, he'd have Liam arrested and interrogated until he revealed the whereabouts of Annie. He'd send Special Forces to rescue her in the dead of night and they would be reunited before morning.

He hadn't left the house, though. Instead, he sat in the living room and watched Liam and the boys eat fish and chips washed down with cheap lager. There was a brief argument over who was entitled to eat his battered sausage but Liam sorted it by pulling rank. The boys were obviously in total awe of him and it sent a shiver through Cormac that he'd once been in exactly the same position as them.

By the time they turned sixteen, there was a definite split within the three musketeers. Harry had long grown tired of Liam's bullying and political ranting. He told Cormac he no longer wished to be associated with Liam. Liam grew to despise Harry for his lack of interest in the only thing that truly mattered to him. So Cormac was piggy in the middle. He'd see Harry on one day, where they'd listen to music and talk about girls, and on another day he'd be with Liam, who was impossibly well read on Irish history and politics for a boy of his age. Liam's house was always full of books. It also had a mysterious quality about it that Cormac could never quite get to grips with. Often, when he was there, the door to the room they were occupying would be hastily shut. They'd hold their ears against the barrier and try, with no success, to make sense of the muffled footsteps and hushed voices of the newly arrived strangers. Liam would educate him about Ireland's plight, about her tragedy and about the wrongs bestowed upon her by her powerful neighbour. Cormac always left those conversations with feelings of great pain and anger that he should be imprisoned in his own country by this cruel foreign aggressor. He had borrowed Liam's books and devoured them by torchlight late into the night in the little room upstairs. Despite Harry's constant warnings, by the time he was eighteen, Cormac was already lost in the romanticism and necessity of the Republican armed struggle. He saw it as the only credible weapon Ireland possessed in the centuries old quest to attain independence from England. With nothing else to balance the incessant drip feed of Republican propaganda, it was inevitable as to where this particular pathway would lead him.

Cormac finished his water and went to find Liam.

He found him where he had left him, holding court in his mother's living room, sitting behind his father's kitchen table. His two disciples sat obediently, peeping up at him from his mother's settee, and nodding like pet puppies. He didn't acknowledge Cormac as he entered the room.

'Have you told me everything I need to know? All I have to do is to answer this phone tomorrow at eight o clock?'

He raised his eyes, but not his head, which was resting on his bruised knuckle.

'Well, technically, you don't even have to answer it. Just have it in your possession in that room at eight. I'll track you to the exact spot and when I am satisfied you are in position, I'll do the rest. If that phone is not in the position it should be, or if you're not with it, then your daughter will die and I'll make sure it is slow and she knows exactly why she is dying. Anything that gives me cause for suspicion will result in her death.'

Cormac walked to the table.

'How do I know that you won't kill her anyway, just for the thrill you so obviously get from it?'

He stood up and walked around the table so that Cormac was staring at the underside of his chin.

'I told you. I have no interest in killing Annie. I used to watch her go to school. I was there when she had her first drink on her 16th birthday, when you couldn't make the party. I watched her having swimming lessons on the weekends when I was around. I have watched her sitting bored in her bedroom for hours, while you sat downstairs drinking wine at your laptop. I even spoke to her once last year, when I got too close one night in a pub in Ponteland. To tell you the truth, I couldn't shake her off that night. I think she was somewhat taken by my good looks and charm! I have to say, in the interests of honesty, I'd a room booked there that night and I was sorely tempted. I didn't do it though. I think I always knew one day you would fall into my lap. I couldn't do anything to jeopardise that, now, could I? When I saw how quickly you were climbing that greasy pole of yours, I knew it wouldn't be long until this moment arrived. I couldn't believe my luck when old Mary O'Reilly popped off this week, of all weeks. I knew even a coward like you would not miss your own mammy's funeral. The trip to Dublin threw me, until I saw you with Bernadette Connelly on that wee bridge off O'Connell Street. I was worried for a bit you might not come back, the way you were gawping at her. So this has all been a bit of a rush, but I think you'll agree it's not too shabby an effort!'

'Why didn't you come for me before this?'

He smiled down at Cormac.

'Don't think for a minute I didn't want to. I thought about it every night in the Maze. I only found out you were in Newcastle after you qualified as a barrister. Your name was in some poncy paper, *The Times*, I think it was. I was on the toilet when I read it. I nearly fell off the pot at the thought of it. I mean, both of us go on the same operation and one of us ends up in the Maze and the other one ends up a barrister, how the fuck does that work? Then I hear you're a fucking MP. At this point, I'm thinking this cunt is really taking the piss! As for the ministerial role, well that was the point when, instead of getting angrier, I realised your blind ambition was going to be my salvation one day and lo and behold, here we are in your ma's house, just like we were the night you ruined my life.'

Cormac took a step back to allow himself to inhale anything other than his rancid breath.

'I don't want to talk to you about that night, but you deserved your sentence. Yes, I should have gone to prison for my part, but I was young and I made a terrible mistake. Since that night, I've tried to live my life as a decent human being. I've tried, and I admit, failed on many occasions, to be a force for good in my work. You, though, what have you done but destroy? All of your life has been nothing but bitterness and failure. You went to the Maze because you deserved to go to the Maze. I used my good fortune to try to do something with the rest of my life, while you, like a cancer, just grew bigger and uglier. I'll die tomorrow night as a man who found redemption. You'll die, and I hope it is soon, as nothing more than shit on the bottom of society's shoe. You think you'll die a hero of Ireland, mourned by the masses? You'll die a sad, lonely, psychopathic junkie, in a gutter somewhere, alone and unmourned.'

The force of the blow sent Cormac crashing against the door. His back made the first contact, before his head followed and punched a small hole. He slid to the floor and tasted blood on his tongue. He wiped his mouth and staggered to his feet. Liam was examining his knuckles which appeared to be pouring with blood. For a moment, Cormac was unsure if the blood in his mouth belonged to him or to Liam. He put his hand into his mouth and removed a hard lump from his tongue. He brought it to his face and could see it was part of a tooth that had been dislodged by the impact. Despite the pain, he drew some comfort that the blood, now pooling in his mouth, did not belong to Liam Conlon.

'Do you want to hit me again or are we done here?'

Liam held his hand in front of his chest. Cormac could see at least one, maybe more, of his knuckles were shattered. He moved towards Cormac. His eyes were dancing.

'I'd fucking love to hit you again. I'd love to keep hitting you, until your whole fucking head caved in, but I'm not going to. I'll settle for blowing you to fuck tomorrow night, or as a poor substitute, destroying your world forever by ending your daughter's short life.'

Cormac opened the fractured living room door.

'If we are done, I'd like you and your two lackeys to leave my home. This is a place where decent people have lived their lives. You are not worthy to dwell in such places. If I'm to die tomorrow night, then I don't wish to spend another moment of the time I have left in the presence of filth and scum. Now get out!'

Liam moved behind the kitchen table and sat down. Cormac thought for a second he was to be stuck with him for some time yet. He picked up the holdall and placed it on the table. He filled it with the laptop and other debris from the table. He stood and nodded to the

197

acne brigade and they made for the open door behind Cormac. He brushed past Cormac before stopping at the front door.

'Goodbye, comrade. Enjoy what's left of your life. Oh, and remember, I will be watching!'

He threw the little black object. Cormac fell to his knees to catch it.

The door slammed.

Cormac looked at his watch.

It told him he had twenty-four hours to live.

—⁓—

35

He called Annie again. Her phone was switched off. He called Tom and after some casual small talk asked him if he knew where Maggie and Jack were. Tom said they sometimes took off for trips like this. They could be anywhere in Ireland, Their favourite destinations were Donegal, if it was a short trip, and Mayo for longer ones. His brother sensed his anxiety and offered to come around but he put him off. The last thing he wanted was to involve Tom in this. He told Tom he loved him, he couldn't help it. It bubbled to the surface towards the end of the conversation and was out before he realised what he'd said. His big brother was obviously embarrassed and mumbled something like 'thanks very much' and promptly hung up. He thought about driving to Harry's to tell the big man all about what had happened. For the same reason he didn't tell Tom he couldn't tell Harry. Harry made his own way in the world and he made his. Harry's decisions gave him a life far removed from the mess he'd made. No, Harry did not deserve to be dragged into this. He thought again about calling the PM and telling him everything. All the things he buried a long time ago. It would end his career, of that there was no doubt, and he deserved whatever fate would befall him. He resisted the temptation. He could not take even a small chance he was jeopardising Annie's life by revealing Liam's plans. Instead he settled for ransacking Maggie's house. He told himself he was searching for vital evidence that might lead him to Annie. He suspected he simply wanted to destroy everything she owned. How could his sister be involved in something like this? Someone who professed to be a God-fearing Christian, kidnapping and maybe even killing her own niece, standing by as a complicit witness to the mass murder of innocents and the torture of her own brother? Those thoughts ensured that by the time he crept out of her back door, the inside of the cottage resembled the aftermath of a hurricane.

Now as the light faded on what could be his last night, he was suddenly aware he was hungry. He hadn't eaten all day; not since the half-eaten biscuit at Maggie's. He made his way to his mother's kitchen. When he got there, he realised there was something else he had to do before satisfying his hunger. It took him twenty minutes and nearly cost him his little finger on two occasions, but his father's table now made the little kitchen resemble the one in which his mother had cooked the stew he was now defrosting in the microwave. He ate it slowly and savoured every mouthful: a condemned man eating a dead woman's food.

The tiredness hit him as he got up to leave the table. The lack of sleep in the hotel in Dublin hadn't helped. The events of the day certainly contributed. Time and time again in his life, in moments of great stress, when he'd been frantically revising for exams, or preparing a closing speech in court, sleep would hit him like a hammer. He'd been awakened on more than one occasion by the disgruntled night porter in the law library after he'd fallen into a deep, drooling sleep over some vital piece of research into a crucial point of law in his latest case. Never had he felt like this, though. He thought about crawling into the living room, because he wasn't convinced he would make it up the stairs. He felt like his body was shutting down in segments, beginning with his legs and working rapidly to his head. He managed to stagger up the staircase with the help of the banister. He pushed open the door to his small bedroom and was under the thin quilt and asleep before his head made contact with the soft pillow.

He awoke in darkness to the rhythmic waves of the rain beating against his window. The morning sun had not yet forced its way through the blackness. Instead, the old street lamp outside the window cast eerie shadows all around the room. Her face woke him. Her face tortured his sleep for the first few years after that night, but he hadn't thought of in at least ten years. It was back and more vivid than ever. He lay in the darkness and tried to bury it like he had so many sleepless nights before, but this time, she wouldn't let him. She didn't want to be buried anymore. She wanted to be remembered. He owed it to her to go back. He could never truly move on without going back. All of the running, all of the hiding, where had it gotten him? Only here, back in the room where the whole nightmare began and with less than one day left to live.

He closed his eyes and did something he swore he'd never do; he cast his mind back to the night of March 9th, 1987.

—◌—

36

It was late afternoon as he lay on the bed. Bernadette, who had just turned 18, left to get ready for a birthday dinner with her parents. They'd spent the previous hour lying side by side in the lamplight, listening to music and excitedly discussing how they were going to tell their parents they were engaged to be married. The ring was his present to her, as well as the two cassettes they took turns playing. He bought her 'The Joshua Tree', mainly because he liked U2, and a Greatest Hits album by Randy Crawford, because she never stopped going on to him about this song she'd heard called 'Almaz.' He mentioned it to Tom, who let him have both albums for the price of one. He could still smell the scent of apples from her hair, on the pillow, now she had gone. They hadn't parted on good terms after she interrogated him for the fourth time about why he appeared so distant. He snapped at her. He regretted that now. He lay listening to the U2 album she hadn't bothered to remove before she left. He'd be better tomorrow. Once he got tonight out of the way, everything would go back to normal. He was understandably nervous about tonight. If he'd crossed the threshold on New Year's Day, upstairs in Lalor's, then tonight, he was closing the door behind him. Tonight he was leaving his childhood behind forever. Tonight he was going on his first operation as an IRA volunteer!

His mother had been into the room twice, once to tell him to turn the music down and the second time to tell him his tea was ready. She was less than pleased when he told her he didn't have the stomach for it. Now he was waiting for the moment when he'd hear Liam's car stop outside his window. He was glad Liam was going with him. He was a familiar face to accompany him on this journey into the unknown. It was not a dangerous job, but it was a very important one. The bearded man he had never met before last Tuesday told them that at the briefing. It was only babysitting a bank manager's wife and daughter on the Malone Road. They'd hold them hostage while the real work was undertaken by the other unit at the bank. It was a simple fund-raising operation. In and out in three hours, he said; even if the job was not complete. In and out in three hours and rendezvous at the address he wrote on the back of his cigar packet that was now nestled in Cormac's shirt pocket.

He'd just come out of the bathroom for the third time inside ten minutes when his mother called him to say Liam was outside waiting in the car. She kissed him on his way out and issued her standard warning regarding Liam. He was nervous and apprehensive about the night to follow when he climbed in beside his friend. He said hello to Liam, but did not get any response. Instead, Liam turned the music up to full volume, hit the steering wheel four times and skidded away from the village down the hill towards the lights of Belfast. They were barely out of the village when he lifted his shirt to show him the gun stuffed into his waistband. Cormac's temperature dropped to match that of the glistening steel that flashed against the passing street lights. He asked Liam to stop the car. He told him he'd made a terrible mistake and he wanted to stop before it went too far. Liam told him it had already gone too far.

He was a volunteer and there was no place for cowardice in the IRA. He tried to calm his thumping chest and just about succeeded by the time they pulled into the waste ground on the outskirts of the city. The other car flashed its lights twice and Liam responded in kind. The door opened and he watched the bearded man approach Liam's stolen old Ford. By the time he climbed into the back seat, Cormac's heart was thumping against his ribs so violently he was surprised the man didn't tell him to turn it down along with the music. The man said something about waiting outside the house until they were called in. Balaclavas were to be worn at all times. Conversations with the hostages must be kept to a minimum and no referral to names or places that could be traced back. Liam answered for both of them, before the man shook their hands and said a short prayer. On the ten-minute journey to the house, Cormac played and rewound the same piece of music again and again. It was the only thing he could do to try and bring some familiarity to the situation he'd so stupidly placed himself in. As they reached the front door and the engine died, he promised himself this was his one and only job. He never wanted to feel like this again. In all the books he read, the speeches he listened to, the seminars in which he'd been an enthusiastic participant, nothing prepared him for the sickening feeling he now had in the pit of his stomach. The feeling that what he was about to do was very wrong and could never be undone. He saw a man being violently bundled into the car in front.

He saw the masked man at the door wave to him.

He felt he was suffocating long before he disappeared into the balaclava.

—⚡—

37

He heard her long before he saw her. He'd only just closed the front door and entered the living room, when he heard her distressed sobbing. There was a young woman wearing a white blouse and a black skirt sitting on the chair opposite the door. She had blonde hair tied back behind her head and looked like she'd just arrived home from a long day at the office. The house smelled of garlic and onions and the dining room table, which was directly behind her, was strewn with the remains of a mid-week family dinner. By far his abiding memory of entering the giant cream and brown room was the sound of her sobbing. It sounded at first like the blonde-haired woman was the one crying, but one look at her face suggested steely determination and disgust at their unwelcome intrusion into her home. She was not one who was going to fall apart in front of her unwelcome guests. The noise was instead coming from behind her back. Liam shouted something to the woman, who turned and pulled the child from behind her. She had a mass of curly blonde hair tumbling across her face and ending at her shoulders. He couldn't see her face too clearly, but well enough to see she was as delicate as a porcelain doll. She was still in her school uniform of grey skirt and green jumper. She could have been no more than six years old. She clung to her mother so tightly it was impossible to tell where one ended and the other began. He wanted to comfort her, but instead realised with a sickening clarity he was the cause of her terror. Liam spoke and flashed the long steel at them which drained the colour from the woman and increased the volume of the little girl. He screamed at the mother to shut the child up. When she proved unsuccessful in the task she'd been set, he lunged at them both and tore the child from her grip. Cormac told him to leave them alone, but he wasn't listening and was throwing the child against the staircase that rose along the wall behind him. He grabbed Cormac's shoulder and pushed him after her. The little girl scampered up the stairs, turned left, and darted through a bedroom door. Liam ordered him to follow her and keep her quiet.

When he entered the room, it was in complete darkness. He could hear her familiar whimper emanating from the bed. He flicked the bedside lamp on and it revealed a pink palace of dolls and teddy bears. The walls were full of hand-painted murals and soft clouds. The bed was empty, apart from a small and bedraggled looking teddy bear. Behind the bed, and squeezed into a tiny space in the corner, was the little girl, curled into a small sobbing mass. He sat for a few minutes, unsure of what to do or say. He asked her if she wanted to play 'I spy,' but she didn't respond. He picked up the teddy and sat it down behind the bed next to her. She didn't look up, but instead felt blindly for it and dragged it into the tight ball with her. He told her he was her friend and he was not going to hurt her. He told her he was only going to be here for a very short time and her daddy would be home in a little while, probably in time for a bedtime story.

She stopped sobbing. He told her he wished he had a little sister as brave and as beautiful as her. She climbed onto the bed and brushed her hair off her face. He realised as he looked into her eyes he meant what he'd said about the little sister. He wanted to put his arm around her, to comfort her, but he knew that wouldn't be right. She started to cry again. She said he couldn't be her friend because she was frightened of him. He told her she should never be frightened of him. She told him the mask was scaring her. He made her promise not to tell anyone if he took it off. They shook hands on it. Her hand was tiny and warm in his. She smiled for the first time when she saw his face. She moved closer to him and asked his name. He whispered it in her ear and she whispered hers to him. She said they were proper friends now.

The door pushed open. He looked up from her face to see Liam march in. He shouted something at them. She started to cry and gripped Cormac's arm tightly. Liam raised his hand and Cormac wanted to stop him. He wanted to dive at him. He wanted to throw himself across her, to protect her. Instead, he sat there in a foggy silence and saw two flashes burst from the end of Liam's outstretched hand. He felt her move away from him. His shirt and face were soaked. He looked around for her. He searched for her face in the mess but it was no longer there.

She was gone.

Liam pointed the gun at him and he hoped for a moment he would see the flash again, but he just told him to wait there and he'd be back to deal with him later. He sat in the corrosive silence of her room. He didn't look for her again. His legs lifted him off the bed and started to take him down the stairs, slowly at first but then faster and faster until he was at the front door.

He turned to see the woman on the chair. Her blouse was open and her chest was bare. She was pleading with him to stay and help her. He saw Liam's outstretched hand pointing at him. He forgot about the woman and thought only of himself. The door frame beside his head splintered as he flailed through it and into the cold darkness of the night.

He ran. He didn't know where he was running to. He was just running away. He saw the light in the red box in the distance and put his hand in his shirt pocket. He dropped the coins three times before he connected with the number. The voice told him where to go and he would be picked up in five minutes. He made another call and told them the address. He told them to hurry. He heard the sirens at the same time his transport arrived. He was given clothes to wear and shown the bathroom. He ran the shower. It was too hot. He got in anyway.

The water scorched his skin as he washed her away.

Within an hour, he was standing at the docks at Larne. The stranger who brought him there was angry when he relayed the events of the night. He told him he must lie low for a while before he returned to Ireland. He was angrier when Cormac told him he no longer wished to be a volunteer. He said that was not an option. Cormac insisted he'd rather be dead than ever get involved in anything again. The man asked him to wait for a moment while he made a phone call. When he came back his mood had changed and he was all handshakes and smiles. He told him he was a lucky bastard. The man with the beard liked him. He told him they'd a proposition for him. He could be released from his obligations in return for never returning to Ireland again. He was not to make contact with his friends or family. If he attempted to do so, he, or they, would become legitimate targets. Cormac said he understood and he was given an address of a house in Newcastle-upon-Tyne and fifty pounds. He was instructed never to speak to his new landlord of the events of the evening. His landlord was a distant relative of the man with the beard and would have no part of any of this if he knew the truth. He shook hands on the deal and walked through the gates.

He stood on the deck as the boat took him from one life to another. He stood alone, away from the glares of the other passengers. He was convinced they were all talking about him. He felt they could see the mark on him; the stamp of his evil. He spent the entire journey to Stranraer being tossed and turned by the rough waters that calmed only as the boat reached the sanctity of the shore. There were no trains until morning, so he spent the night on a bench at the station. He arrived in Newcastle the following afternoon and knocked on the door of the tall red brick house in Jesmond. A pretty blonde girl, with kind blue eyes, opened the door to him. She said her father was at a council meeting, but they were expecting him. She told him her name was Jill and she already knew his name. He ate with her and she talked and he listened. He saw the newspaper headline two days later. He picked up the paper and read it in the little shop on the corner.

BUTCHERED: MOTHER AND DAUGHTER SLAIN!

A young mother and her daughter were brutally murdered in what police say was a bungled IRA operation. Mrs Jennifer McCartney, the wife of

Northern Bank manager Peter, suffered what police describe as an horrendous ordeal at the hands of the lone perpetrator, who was apprehended as he was leaving the premises. She sustained a single gunshot wound to the back of the head, although police believe that the 32-year-old solicitor had already died as a result of strangulation. The victim, whose body was discovered at the top of the stairs, had endured a vicious and prolonged sexual assault and had some fifty-seven bite marks on her back and torso. Police believe the young mother was making a desperate attempt to reach her daughter's bedroom. It is understood, however, from the forensic examinations of both victims, that the child, who sustained two gunshot wounds to the face, died before her mother. Chief Superintendent Reg Donaldson commented: 'In all my time serving in the RUC, my officers have never dealt with a more distressing scene. The only small consolation we can take from this tragedy is that the perpetrator has been caught and will be brought to justice. I would like to thank the concerned neighbour who contacted the police to report this incident and if that person would make themselves known to me, I would like to take the opportunity to thank him personally.'

The victims were formally identified as 32-year-old Jennifer Mary McCartney and her 6-year-old daughter Annie.

He felt the water gather in small puddles in his ears, then pour onto the pillow behind his head. He let it flow until no more would come. He raised himself from the bed and opened the old curtains. The first shafts of morning sun were fighting their way through the thick blanket of cloud that hung low over the church on the hill. The room filled with a soft light that banished the shadows that had engulfed it. The water from the rain still meandered its way slowly down the dirty pane. He sat back down on the noisy ancient bed he'd slept in as a child and contemplated the day ahead: the most important day of his life. Maybe the only day left in his life.

By the time he drank the last of his mother's tea, he knew what he had to do. He must sacrifice himself for Annie. This was not a time for running away. He'd done that once before, and where had that gotten him? He was still running twenty-two years later. It would all end today. He must be strong for her; he must be brave for her. He was not a coward. He had been a boy then, but now he was a man. He would sacrifice himself so Annie could live. Annie deserved that from him. He looked at the little black object on the kitchen table. He picked it up and placed it in his trouser pocket.

He was no longer afraid.

—⚏—

38

He squinted and bent over the monitor. The little green dot had definitely moved. The Chemist said it was one hundred per cent accurate. He looked at his watch, which told him it was only 6.20 pm. He felt it was too early and the doubt made him grind his teeth. He asked the boys to have a look and they all studied the screen. He was definitely on his way out of the house. He ordered the boys to their seats and pulled his chair against the table. He felt a sharp surge in his groin as he watched the green dot turn right and begin its descent towards Belfast. He'd always wondered what this day would feel like. He hoped he could stay calm and in control; a cool, brilliant puppet master, pulling on the strings of history. As he watched the dot pass onto the motorway that would take it to Hillsborough Castle, he realised he could not be calm about something as monumental as this. Cormac O'Reilly was heading towards his target and he was only fifteen minutes away from his destination. In less than two hours, Cormac would be in the exact position. The green dot would gently move across his screen until it finally settled on top of the little red dot that indicated precisely where the banqueting hall was situated. He would then make one call and the dot would vanish from the screen forever! He watched it move past Finaghy and then Dunmurry. When it by-passed Lisburn, he could hardly contain the burning sensations in his groin and stomach. He opened the drawer, took out the packet and sniffed it frantically and messily up his nose. It burned and nearly made him sneeze. He held his nose until the urge had passed. He looked at the screen and saw the dot leave the motorway at Hillsborough. The buzz in his head threatened to blow the roof of the cramped room. He didn't even register the fact he was standing now, punching the air and screaming at the top of his lungs. Nothing had ever felt this good before! He forced himself to breathe slowly when he saw the dot enter the grounds of the Castle. The clock on the screen flashed 6:50 p.m. He was early, but not too early. The dot was moving very slowly now. At the left edge of the screen he saw the tiny red glow emerge. He bit his hand so hard his blood dripped slowly onto the keyboard. He paused to watch it trickle and fall between the keys.

By 7:15 p.m., he was beginning to get concerned. The dot had not moved at all for fifteen minutes. The Chemist said it would be possible to identify even the smallest of movements. He said even if someone was walking around in the same room, the dot would move too. It hadn't moved. It was positioned just to the right of the red dot but not quite on it. He told himself to calm down; that Cormac was probably in the room next door enjoying pre- dinner drinks.

He waited.

At 7:30 p.m., he was very concerned.

He waited.

At 7:45 p.m., he called Jack.

He gave the order because he simply couldn't trust Cormac. He promised him he wouldn't do it until

8:05 pm, but he simply didn't like the look of that stationary green dot on the screen. If Cormac was going to mess him about, then he was going to pay. He hung up and poured a vodka in honour of Annie. It wasn't her fault her father was a coward right till the end. He sat in front of the screen. It flashed 7:53 p.m.

The buffet banquet was in full glorious flow. The Queen arrived at 7:50 p.m. through the Great Doors that opened to the right of the platform where the Ulster Youth Orchestra was enjoying its proudest moment, playing Vivaldi to Her Majesty and other distinguished guests. Her Majesty's arrival caused a great stir, even amongst the battle-weary old statesmen in the room. All eyes were firmly fixed on her, apart from the two men who slipped unnoticed to the far end of the room and now stood, framed in the large oval window, staring at the bustling but discreet activity in the distance.

At 8 p.m., he picked up the phone, more in hope than expectation. The green dot hadn't moved its position on the screen since it settled to the right of the red dot at 7 p.m. He knew deep in his gut Cormac hadn't kept to the agreement. The conversation with Jack at 7:55 p.m. was some small consolation. Mission accomplished, he'd said. Annie O'Reilly was an unfortunate casualty of war and of her own father's cowardice. He dialled the number and watched as the green dot disappeared from the screen.

No one in the room registered the dull thud which was audible over Vivaldi and the hum of excited conversation. The two men watched the small flash dislodge the first layer of sandbags. An army of ants quickly moved in to begin the efficient work of clearing the debris, before the guests arrived on the terrace for post-banquet drinks to the accompaniment of Ireland's premier solo harpist. Cormac turned to the older man, who was anxiously reading from his BlackBerry.

'When can I speak with Annie, Prime Minister?'

The door to the upstairs room at Lalor's crashed to the floor with a deafening bang. He hadn't had time to put the phone back onto the desk before the first burst of automatic fire ripped through his neck and chest. The second burst hit him on his left shoulder and sent him swaying to the right. The third and fourth bursts, which tore the right side of his jawbone off and ripped into his gut, ensured he was dead long before he finished the dance and smashed his mutilated head against the blood spattered wall.

The two boys died where they sat transfixed in their chairs. One was armed with an ancient revolver, the other with a can of Diet Coke.

Cormac watched the Prime Minister's phone light up. The old man turned his back to him and took two short paces away from him. When he turned, he tried to speak, but no words came out of his mouth. He put his hand on Cormac's shoulder.

'I am so very sorry, son, I....'

Cormac knew he couldn't let him finish. He wouldn't let him finish.

'No! I don't want to hear it! I don't want to hear what you have to say to me! You promised me ... you promised me as a friend she was safe. You said you spoke to her! At four o' clock today, you told me you spoke to her! I wouldn't have gone through with it, but you told me she was safe. So don't you fucking dare tell me you are sorry. Don't!'

The old man walked him to the doors of the great hall to prevent the small number who were staring from growing any larger. Once outside, the Prime Minister fumbled for the bench that sat at the top of the great staircase. He opened his shirt to stem the flow of sweat gathering on his forehead. Cormac slid down the wall next to him.

'Why? Why did you lie to me? You, of all people. I trusted you. You're supposed to be my friend.'

The old man spoke through his fingers that now appeared to be trying to block his words from finding their way through.

'It was not my decision, Cormac. This was bigger than all of us. I was told they located the area where they thought she was being held, but it was a false alarm. By then, it was too late to alter anything. I have hoped and prayed all day they would find her, but they didn't. Not until it was too late.

'What happened?'

The old man did not respond.

'How did my daughter die?'

'There was an explosion in a car on a country road near Enniskillin. Your brother-in-law was arrested close to the scene. He confessed he'd been acting on orders received at 7:45 p.m. from his Commanding Officer. He said he was a volunteer of the True Irish Republican Army. Cormac, I know you can never forgive me. Your beautiful child is dead. Oh, Christ, Cormac! Little Annie is dead!'

—⁓—

39

He was still speaking but Cormac couldn't hear any words. It was as if the prime minister's voice was passing though water before it reached his ears. He knew he wanted to get up from his position on the floor, but his brain was not firing any signals to the rest of his body. He turned to look at the old man, he was still sitting on the bench, but he seemed to be moving away from him. He looked around the great hallway for something solid to focus on, but the walls and the giant staircase appeared to be liquid. He used all of his energy to push his back against the wall. He rose unsteadily to his feet. The sounds began to creep back. He could hear the music and chatter from next door. The orchestra sounded like it had forgotten how to play. The laughter in the room was mocking him. He saw two red-faced men on the stairs pointing at him, talking about him; laughing at him. He tried to shout to them, to walk towards them, but he merely staggered off the wall and fell to the floor like a drunk who'd been hit for the final time in a bar-room brawl. Then there was blackness.

When he regained consciousness, there was a small group of faces staring down at him. For one glorious moment, he forgot why they would be making such a fuss, until her face flashed before him. His little girl, smiling at him, laughing and then gone. Gone because of what he had done. Damned before she was even born. Dead so he could live. He had saved himself, and in doing so sacrificed his only child. The pain of the thought was too much to bear and he felt the room begin to swirl and the darkness descend again. He had to get up. He had to get out of here. He had to go to her. He pulled himself up with the help of the chair and a bejewelled arm, and started to walk towards the staircase. He held the banister and stumbled and staggered his way to the bottom. He fell through the front doors and arrived into a beautiful summer evening. He looked to the sky and didn't understand. He didn't understand how the sun could still shine. How could the sun shine when all the light had left his world? He walked into the gardens and fell to his knees in the dirt of the shrubbery. He tore at his shirt. He called her name. He screamed her name! He begged her to hear him, but she didn't answer his cry.

When the ringing in his head had subsided, it was replaced by a buzzing in his chest. Then the buzzing in his chest stopped for a second and started again. It stopped and started three more times, before his brain collated it was the phone in his jacket pocket vibrating against him. He searched in his pocket to find it. He readied himself to throw it as far away as he could. He looked at the screen through raw eyes and snapped to his senses - *MAGGIE!*

He pushed the green button and slapped the phone to his ear.

'How could you do it? You're my sister, for fuck's sake. She was my child. How could you do that to Annie? Do you hate me that much? You evil bitch - you'll get what's coming....'

She tried to speak, but he wouldn't let her.

'Where are you hiding? I'm coming to get you. You better hope the police get to you first!'

She was shouting now, screaming and crying down the phone. He paused.

'Will you calm down and listen for a minute?'

He didn't want to listen to her, not to her reasons and her pathetic excuses.

'I won't listen to you. Where are you?'

She was bellowing now.

'It's Maggie! It's Maggie!'

He didn't want to hear her name. She killed his child. She may not have been the one to do it but she was as guilty as Jack, or Liam.

'I don't want to hear your name ever again, you evil bitch. I never want to hear your name again!'

There was silence on the other end of the line, and then she spoke through her tears.

'It's Maggie, she's dead. Dad, please listen. It's me, Annie! Dad, please, I need you to listen to me. It's me. I'm all right.'

He stood up from where he was crouching. He was listening now.

'Dad, are you still there?'

He recognised her voice now. He didn't answer because he wanted her to speak again. He wanted her to speak and never stop speaking again!

'Dad, Maggie took my place. She knew, Dad. She knew something was wrong and she took my place. She took my coat and drove the car instead of me. He thought it was me in the car, but she wouldn't let me go. She died for me. Maggie died for me!'

She was sobbing uncontrollably now.

He wanted to reach through the phone and grab her and never let her go.

'Annie! Oh, Annie! I thought you were dead. I thought I'd never hear your voice or see your face again. Annie, I thought Maggie was part of it. All those things I said, I thought she was responsible for your death. Christ! Poor Maggie! Where are you? I'm coming to get you!'

Her voice was steady now.

'It's alright Dad. I'm on my way back to Killane now with the police. I'll be there in an hour. I'll meet you there.'

He couldn't think of anything else to say.

'Annie.'

'What?'

'Guess what?'

As he walked to the car, he looked up at the grand old castle. He saw an old man gazing at him from the last oval window on the second floor. Cormac raised his right hand to him and saw him smile. He got into the hire car and looked in the mirror. He was unrecognisable. His eyes were red glows sat deeply in a muddy mess. He smiled to no one and left the political establishment to their Champagne and canapés and drove off in search of happiness. The relief and exhilaration that his daughter was still living and breathing carried him all the way to Belfast. When he turned left to drive the short distance uphill to Killane, only then did he feel the loss of Maggie stab at his chest. He saw the commotion at Lalor's as he drove into the village. Two police cars flanked the ambulance that was swallowing the third and largest of the black body bags. He turned left and brought the car to a halt outside his mother's house. When he left this place three hours ago, he absolutely believed he would live, Annie would be safe and Liam Conlon would be gone forever. He achieved everything he set out to achieve. Yet as he started to walk towards the old front door, he felt the stabbing in his chest again. He turned and looked up the hill. He saw the church steeple silhouetted against the darkening night sky. He thought of Maggie. Maggie, who he thought was the enemy, who only three hours ago, he was sure he would not have mourned; Maggie, who sacrificed her life so they could have theirs. He closed the rusty gate behind him and strolled towards the church on the hill. He would light a candle for Maggie. She would want him to do that for her.

He wanted to do that for her.

—⚏—

40

The latch clicked loudly as Cormac forced the giant iron ring as far as it would rotate. The door held for a second before succumbing to the pressure of his shoulder. Its ancient hinges groaned as he stepped noisily into the empty darkness of the foyer.

The doors to the chapel were more welcoming and he passed through with a gentle swish. They were still rocking gently to a standstill by the time he walked the short distance to the little altar. He stood where only days ago, his mother's coffin lay while ritual and ceremony sent her on her way. His mother and father had knelt on the ground, on the altar in front of him, on their wedding day. His mother knelt here last Sunday, blissfully unaware that what she had always referred to as her mortal toil was all but over. He slid into the front pew, at the end of which he could see a single row of candles. Only one was glowing, and he was glad of that. He would use it to light a candle for Maggie and spend a few moments just thinking of her. He wouldn't pray for her, because that would make him a hypocrite. He would think of her, though. The life she led that was so very different from his own. He envied her the certainty she possessed that there was a better place than this. This little church was the centre of her universe. She was baptised here, and like him made her first confession and communion here also. After those rites of passage, this place began to mean less and less to him. It was a place he endured for one tortuous hour every Sunday. It was only made tolerable by the thought there would be a delicious roast dinner on the table as soon as he called at Lalor's to tell his dad and Tom their worship was over for the day as well. On some Sundays, he'd show his face at the door of the church, pick up a news sheet and dash off with Harry over the hill to play football until he saw the congregation make their way towards him. No, this place did not mean much to Cormac - yet as he sat in the darkness, he realised it remained part of him. His whole history was in this place: christenings, communions, confirmations, marriages, deaths. There had even been the ordination of his uncle Damien here. Cormac watched, as an awe struck ten-year-old, as his uncle lay prostrate on the altar while the bishop called him to serve his heavenly father. Damien's passion for Christ unfortunately did not compare to his passion for altar boys and he vanished from his parish in Armagh and was never spoken of again in Cormac's house.

He hadn't noticed it at the funeral, but the smell was still the same. It smelled of rotting wood and sweat, but not in a bad way - rather in a way that spoke to him of his lost innocence. He closed his eyes and inhaled it deeply into his lungs, like he was trying to store it there. He knew he was breathing it in because he'd already decided he would never return here. It was part of his childhood, but it had no place in his future.

He heard a faint sound coming from the left of the altar and looked up, startled. Out of the darkness came the little parish priest. Fr. Mackie had been here nearly as long as the church. He had baptised Cormac. He was also the first teacher to hit him with a ruler when he failed to recite the Ten Commandments to his satisfaction. He'd been a keen sportsman, a footballer and Gaelic footballer, in his time. He had a soft lilting West of Ireland accent and used to talk so fondly of his home in Achill Island that Cormac always wondered why he didn't just go back there to live. After the caning episode, he sincerely wished he would! The shuffling frailty of his gait, as he approached the centre of the altar, suggested a man who'd never heard of, or hadn't been informed of, the retirement age. He still had his hair, but rather than the thick jet-black thatch of his youth, it was now thin wisps of white that Cormac surmised wouldn't survive a gentle gust. As he stooped to bless himself in front of the altar, Cormac could see it wouldn't be long before the old priest occupied his mother's position directly behind where he now struggled to stand up. He turned and walked past Cormac to where the lone candle was burning. He took one from a box and struggled to hold it still enough to light it off the flame. His tangled hand vibrated from side to side and each time narrowly missed the small flame.

'Can I help you with that, Father?'

He shuffled around to face Cormac and was not at all fazed by the stranger in his midst. He was a man who'd gotten used to repentant sinners frequenting his church at all hours of the day. He studied the general area from where the voice had come.

'Yes, if you don't mind, son. My old hands aren't what they used to be and I really would like to light this candle for a dear friend of mine and a beautiful soul who's passed on to a better place tonight.'

Cormac walked towards him until he was within his range. He saw the look of recognition in his almost hidden eyes.

'Cormac, is that you, son?'

Cormac took the candle from him and lit it from the dying flame.

'Yes, Fr. Mackie it's me. I came to light a candle for Maggie. I won't be long till I am gone.'

He pointed a crooked finger towards the candle.

'You just did, my son. That's what I was trying to do myself, you see.'

Cormac sat down on the uncomfortable bench. The priest stood. Cormac could tell he wanted to speak, but couldn't find the words. He was about to fill the void when Fr. Mackie began.

'Cormac, I'm so pleased you've come to me. You see, if you hadn't, I'm afraid I wouldn't have possessed the courage to find you, and I must speak with you about your sister.'

The old priest was trembling so much, Cormac took his arm and guided him into the seat next to him.

'Maggie came to see me the day after your mother's funeral. She was very upset and confused. She knew Jack had been mixing with a bad crowd, but she was never sure to what extent his involvement stretched - until she overheard him on the phone. She feared for your safety and for your daughter. She was tormented because she knew something, yet nothing at all.'

Cormac interrupted him.

'Why didn't she go to the police?'

'I told her to go to the police immediately, but she was a stubborn woman, Maggie O'Reilly, and like I say, at that stage, she knew something but maybe nothing at all. Her only concern when she left here was to protect you and your daughter.'

Cormac thought of the names he had called her on the phone to Annie and the thoughts he had harboured last night after Liam had told him she was involved. He turned away from the priest for fear he would see his shame.

'She did a very brave thing for me, Father. Something I'm not sure I deserved from her. I'll never forget what she did and never understand it.'

'Nonsense, son, your mother and Maggie would never let a week go by without telling me every detail of what Cormac O' Reilly was up to in England. They had you as the next prime minister the day you first set foot in Parliament. She was very proud of you and she died because of her love for you.'

They sat in silence, Cormac thinking and the priest praying. Cormac stood up to leave. The priest moved his arm faster than Cormac thought possible for him. He pulled Cormac onto the bench.

'Son, there's something else I have to say. It is something I promised your mother I would never disclose, but now she is gone, I have to unburden myself of it. I told Maggie of what we did, but now she has passed, I want to tell you.'

The old man started to shake again.

'We took her child, your mother and me. We took her child and God forgive me, it was not ours to take. We thought we were helping her. We thought we were giving her a life, but all we were doing was hiding your family's shame. Your mother couldn't face the shame, so we destroyed your sister before she even had a chance to live. She would come to me and pray for her lost child and all the while I'd know I'd stolen it from her. I was her priest and her confidante and all these years I was lying to her. I don't know if even my all merciful God can forgive me.'

The tears were rolling down his wizened cheeks.

'I told her this when she came to see me after the funeral. I told her what me and your dear misguided mother did to her when she was just a child herself.'

The old man stood up and fumbled in his pocket.

'And do you know what she said to me? She said she forgave me! Oh merciful Jesus! She looked me in the eye and thanked me for telling her. Then we prayed together, one last time for her lost child, before I could take no more.'

He began to shuffle past Cormac and dropped a folded envelope onto the floor as he passed.

Cormac stretched through a tight gap in front of him to reach it.

'Father, you've dropped this.'

He didn't turn around.

'No, son, I didn't drop it. I was hoping you wouldn't see it until I left.'

He heard the door gently close. He looked at the front of the envelope. It contained two words scrawled in barely legible black ink: *FOR CORMAC*.

He slid across the bench until he reached the light from her candle. He unfolded the small square from inside. He held it in the light and began to read.

Dear Cormac,

I know if you are ever reading this then it means I am gone. I'm not much of a writer as will be apparent to you from this. I'm writing this in the presence of Fr. Mackie who has just told me what happened to my child all those years ago. I wanted to write to you because I know I've not always, or ever in fact, behaved like a sister to you. I know on many an occasion when you were just a boy I made your life a misery. I do not ask your forgiveness for my cruelty, I only ask that you understand. I was angry and bitter at the loss of my baby and I took that anger out on you. It was not your fault. Your only crime was to be a constant reminder to me of what I lost. I want you to know I've always loved you and I've always been very proud of your achievements. I'm going to leave you in peace now Cormac. It is with great pain but also great pride I now know the truth. The child I thought I'd lost all those years ago was in fact with me every day. I only wish I could have loved you more. Forgive me for the sentimentality of the next line. I've waited my whole life to say it but I'll have to settle for writing it.

Good night and God bless, my son.
Your loving mother,
MAGGIE xxx

He could hardly read the last three lines through the saturated paper. He sat the letter down beside him.

He fell off the bench and onto his knees.

And prayed to a God he didn't believe in, for a mother he never knew.

—ጢ—

41

The disgraced former minister walked from the warmth and light and stepped into the cold and dark. His shoulders ached and he paused for a moment to adjust his grip before finding a sanctuary in a little doorway of a derelict shop front. He'd never been happier or more content.

He sat his bags on the damp ground next to a young man in a blanket who wasn't particularly impressed he'd trespassed on his patch. The boy's mood softened when he placed ten pounds in his cup and wished him a Merry Christmas. Cormac turned his collar to the biting wind and relentless drizzle. He could hear Shane McGowan and Kirsty McColl drifting in the strong breeze as it whistled past him along with the huge throng of Christmas shoppers. He raised his gaze and studied the castle which stood proudly on its rock and had defied this weather and more over the previous centuries. It was lit up like a Christmas tree in the darkness of this December afternoon. Through the crowds swimming past his face, he could make out the German market stalls across the street. He studied the little open-air bar, where weary shoppers sat buttoning their coats to keep the chill off their bodies whilst at the same time poured pints of freezing liquid down their throats to warm their spirits.

At the far end of the tiny counter, he saw the big man engaged in warm conversation with a group of twenty-something men all dressed as superheroes. Harry Crossan had never changed in all this time, and Cormac hoped he never would. He felt a pang of regret he hadn't spent more time with him over the years. The past few months made up for it in some small way. The two old friends met in Edinburgh on four or five occasions on the premise of visiting Annie and Claire, but in reality, it was a way of spending some time together. There'd been other occasions as well. After the resignation, when the newspaper headlines were at their most lurid and hurtful, they'd retreated to Harry's place in Nice. Cormac enjoyed the blissful anonymity so much, he'd seriously considered Harry's offer to move there on a permanent basis. Everything had changed, though. Everything utterly changed over the course of one very drunken conversation.

Harry told him she was no longer with the English professor. He returned less than a month after they left for America. The move was the last desperate attempt to save a marriage already beyond repair. He knew what he had to do in the instant Harry told him. His stomach turned a full circle and back again and his fingers and toes had buzzed like they'd been plugged in to the mains. He decided in his drunken stupor he would go to her and tell her how he felt about her. He would make her see it was not too late to start over again. They were young and still had a lifetime to live. Why couldn't they share it with each other? Harry was a reluctant detective for him. He was not on great speaking terms with Roisin and Marcus, who spent most of their time and a lot of Harry's money on travelling between the apartment in

New York and the villa in Bermuda. Harry eventually established she was working as a writer in a theatre somewhere on Broadway, or just off it. He could not find out, no matter how hard he tried, where she was living.

When Cormac had finally sold the farmhouse for a painfully low price last week, he decided the time was right to go, even on what little information he had. The bags at his feet were the result of his guilt at leaving Annie at such short notice. He put a box under each arm and wrapped his freezing fingers around the rest. He said goodbye to the relieved boy in the blanket and waited five minutes for a gap in the masses before he pushed his way across the street to join Harry, who was in earnest conversation with Batman, Robin and a swaying Spiderman.

'Ah, Cormac! Tell these youngsters here who wrote 'The First Cut is the Deepest.' Batman here thinks it was Rod Stewart and Robin thinks it was P.P. Arnold. Now I have told them, whilst there is no doubt Rod did a good version of it, P.P.'s was much better. However, the bloody thing was written by old Yusuf Islam himself, aka Cat Stevens, now am I right, my friend, or am I right?'

Cormac grinned to himself as he pointed out to the forty-something superheroes that looked twenty something from a distance, his big friend was always right, except on the odd occasion when he couldn't actually remember the question he had asked. Harry shook his hand in puzzled gratitude for the endorsement. They left them just as Batman and Robin were wasting all their superpowers in a vain attempt to revive Superman, who was face down on the counter of the small stall. When they lifted him, his face was smeared in what Cormac was sure was thick dark blood. His fears were eased when he saw Spiderman scrape Superman's cheek with a spoon and dress his giant hot- dog with it.

He stopped, for the second time in two minutes, to rest his aching arms.

'Jesus, Cormac, will you give me some of those bags. You've got more presents there than Santa!'

He was grateful for Harry's giant hands. The rest of the short journey, he walked, excitedly anticipating Annie's surprise when she saw him at her front door. By the time they reached the Georgian terrace, his excitement turned to dread at the thought of what he was about to tell her. That he was leaving her in less than an hour's time and he didn't know when, or if, he would be returning. He would be in New York by tomorrow morning on a one-way ticket. They stood on the front step. He banged his fist on the door.

It was drowned by the thumping bass booming from the other side.

It was another five minutes before the door was opened and even then it was more by chance than any design. A lanky boy, with too much hair on his head and face, pushed past them and made it to the fence, before projecting the liquid contents of his stomach over the pavement on the other side. Cormac checked his watch, which told him it was 5:20 p.m. The boy wiped his mouth on his grey sweatshirt before making his way back towards them.

He spoke with a slurred Yorkshire accent.

'Sorry about that, chaps. It must've been something I ate. Can I help you, gentlemen? Oh fuck, you're not the police, are you? I mean, not that there is a problem if you are the police. It's just you look a bit old for the party, what with the matching trench coats and all that. Are you Mormons, then? I suppose you could be Mormons. You look a bit like the two blokes who used to come to our house and they were Mormons. Or were they Jehovah's Witnesses? If you are Jehovah's Witnesses, I wouldn't be going in there it'll scar you for life!'

He grimaced at Cormac.

'No, you don't look like a Jehovah's Witness, but you're definitely much too short to be a Mormon! Then you must be selling something and if you are, you can fuck right off! That is unless you are actually the police, in which case, I'm very sorry for swearing at you, officer.'

'Dad, what are you doing here?'

She stood framed in the doorway. Her flowing red hair was gone and was replaced by a shorter style bob that framed her delicate pale face and made her look five years older than her eighteen years. She was wearing trainers, jeans and a sweat top, which matched the now blessedly quiet irritant that had momentarily disappeared from Cormac's field of vision.

She hugged him before he could answer and poured the contents of what looked like a bottle of antifreeze she was holding down the inside of his coat. He wanted to jump with the shock of it, but he decided to hold on to her for a little longer instead. She pulled herself away from him and flung her arms around Harry. Then she pushed past them so she could reach the drunken hairy boy who was standing ashen-faced behind them.

'There you are! I've been searching everywhere for you.'

She slipped her hand into his and walked him to Cormac.

He suddenly wished he hadn't called at the flat at all.

'Dad, this is Mark, my boyfriend I was telling you about on the phone.'

He suppressed the sigh that was fighting to get out and instead offered his hand.

'Pleased to meet you, Mark, I'm Cormac.'

The boy looked him in the eye, slipped his hand from Annie's, and shook Cormac's hand warmly.

'It's very nice to finally meet you, Mr O'Reilly. Annie has told me a lot about you. In fact, she never shuts up about you.'

He quickly averted his gaze to focus on the bags on the top step.

'Can I help you with your bags Mr O'Reilly? You and Annie will have a lot to catch up on, so if it's alright with you, I'll take these upstairs and be out of your way.'

Cormac looked at him as he frantically tried to scurry past them and up the narrow staircase. He was no more than eighteen years old, and if he'd half of his hair removed and several good dinners inside him, he could pass for very handsome. Annie had spoken incessantly about him in their recent telephone conversations. He thought of him throwing up in the garden and of the complete gibberish he and Harry had been subjected to and compared it to his own activities at a similar age. He shivered at the thought and quickly banished it. The boy was nearly past him when he caught his arm.

'It's very nice to meet you too, Mark. Please call me Cormac, as I think we have a lot in common.'

He stopped, and the fear had left his face.

'Oh, what's that then?'

'It appears that Annie here never stops talking about the both of us!'

He felt a sharp pain in his shin and was glad she was wearing trainers. Mark smiled at him as they followed him up the stairs. He turned as he reached the top and shouted over the noise.

'Hey, Cormac!'

'What?'

'I knew you were too short to be a Mormon!'

—ɷ—

42

The noise stopped as soon as they entered the crowded living room. It started immediately again, once those who were still coherent established they weren't actually the police. Cormac glanced around the room he'd furnished with Annie only three months previously. It was unrecognisable. Every space on the wall was covered with all manner of posters, advertising anything from bands he'd never heard of, to theatre shows he'd never seen, to obscure films requiring degree level French or German to be fully appreciated. The two neat settees he'd bought were draped in what looked like Indian saris and were now accompanied by several beanbags of various shapes and sizes. Every available space was occupied by boys who appeared to be cloned from Mark and equally as drunk, or girls who looked severely malnourished and swigged the same blue liquid now adhering his shirt to his back. The music was unrecognisable to him; all bass and drumbeats.

He looked at Harry, who was cuddling Claire under his giant arm.

'Do you know the music, Harry?'

The big man shook his head.

'No I don't, and you know the old saying, don't you, my friend?'

Cormac shook his head.

'If you don't know the music, you're at the wrong party!'

'Whose old saying is that, then?'

Harry smiled and pointed towards Annie in the kitchen.

'I think it's actually one of mine. Forget the music though, by my watch, we've about half an hour before we have to shoot off. I think you need to speak with Annie, don't you?'

Cormac turned, and after five minutes of trying to plan the pathway of least resistance to her through the mass of bodies in his way and another minute in executing the plan, he was standing next to Annie, who was busy pouring two drinks into dirty pint glasses. She handed one to Cormac.

'This really is a great surprise, Dad. I didn't think I would get to see you again until Christmas. I can't wait to spend some time with you at the farm, just the two of us together again.'

He felt his heartbeat quicken.

'We can lock ourselves away. Go on some of those long walks I used to hate as a child but now can't wait to do. We can even have a couple of days away together if you like?'

He sat the glass on the crowded bench and swallowed hard. There was no easy way to tell your child you'd sold the only home she ever knew, or you were breaking your promise to spend Christmas with her. There certainly was no easy way to inform her you were running off to America and were hoping you didn't have to come back.

'What is it, Dad? You look like you're about to faint. Are you all right?'

He looked into her pale blue eyes and thought of how he'd so nearly lost her for good. He'd nearly lost her and yet here he was about to leave her. For a moment, he just couldn't do it. How could he break her heart like this?

He felt his eyes water. She spoke before he found the courage.

'Dad, I'm a big girl and I'm happy for you. Claire told me last week. I wish you'd told me sooner. I thought you were going to go without saying a proper goodbye. It was a bit of a shock at first, but I think you're doing the right thing. I want you to be happy wherever you are. I'll be alright. I'll miss you so much, but I'll phone every night, even if it's just so I can hear you say, 'guess what, Annie?' I have heard that so much in my life, I don't ever want to live without it.'

She moved away from him and held his hand to her chest.

'It's all in here, Dad. No matter where you are, you'll always be in here. I think that makes me a very lucky girl, don't you?'

He lifted his hands to her face and used his thumbs to stem the tide freely flowing down her cheeks. He pulled her to him.

'I don't know how you managed to turn out like this, Annie. I think it was in spite of my efforts rather than because of them. I was always too....'

She put her finger to his lips.

'Stop it, Dad. Yes, sometimes you had to work and occasionally you missed a school play or something and sometimes I'd see the other kids with their mums and feel a little jealous of them. It hasn't really been till I came here that I realised how lucky I was, when I hear all the sad stories of ruined childhoods. Every day you made me feel loved - like I was the most special girl in the world. I never thanked you for that, for the love you gave me. Your whole life has been about me, now it's time for you to live just for you. If that Bernadette one isn't smart enough to see what she is missing, I'll go to New York myself and sort her out for you. When do you have to leave?'

'He has to leave now, Annie.'

Harry was standing in the doorway, still clutching Claire.

He hugged her once more in the street.

He looked back to see her and Mark wave before she closed the door.

They didn't speak much on the flight to London or in the lounge where Harry waited with him until his flight was called. Now it had been, they spoke in a rush. Yes, I'll come and visit. No, Roisin's not using the apartment. No I don't want rent. No, I don't know where Bernadette lives. Yes, I have the address. Yes, I know it's walking distance from Broadway. Yes, I know Broadway's a big place.

The tannoy announced last call. They walked to the gate. The old friends embraced each other. He thought the big man was going to crush his ribs. He searched for something poignant or memorable to mark the occasion, but it wouldn't come. Instead, he walked through the gate and then he remembered. He shouted back beyond the impatient queue behind him.

'Hey Harry, who sang 'I Wanna Kiss You All Over'?

The big man put his hand to his ear to signal he couldn't hear him.

'Shout louder, Cormac!'

He shouted.

'I WANNA KISS YOU ALL OVER!'

They were staring now.

'I don't know. Can you sing a bit of it for me?'

He looked around him. The queue had lost interest. He sang a bit.

> *'I wanna kiss you all over*
> *Over again*
> *I wanna kiss you all over*
> *Till the night closes in....'*

Harry still had his hand to his ear.

'I've nearly got it. Sing a bit more if you can and a bit louder.'

He sang in a shout.

> *'Stay with me, lay with me*
> *Holding me, loving me*
> *Ba...a...by.'*

The queue rediscovered its interest and now formed a circle around him waiting for Harry's response. He leaned around the counter and called Cormac to him. Cormac bent his ear to Harry's cupped hand.

'It was Exile, Cormac. Exile sang it. Oh, and by the way, I knew the answer on the 'who sang, "I wanna kiss you all over"' bit, because I'm the daddy when it comes to music, I think you'll agree. Now if you'd like to turn around, my gullible friend, your audience awaits.'

He clapped his hands as Cormac began to move and the audience joined in rapturously. Cormac fixed his gaze firmly on the floor and didn't look up, even when he heard the gruff American accent ask Harry who actually sang the song. He was walking quickly down the tunnel when he heard his friend's theatrical reply, delivered in a camp style any method actor would be proud of.

'I'M SORRY, SIR, BUT I'M TOO UPSET TO ANSWER THAT QUESTION! YOU SEE, THAT OLD DOG THERE BROKE MY HEART AND NOW HE WANTS TO RUB MY NOSE IN THE DIRT! OH, THIS IS ALL SO DREADFULLY PAINFUL!'

It wasn't until he was in his seat Cormac allowed himself a smile at his own stupidity. He was glad Harry Crossan was his friend and he was sure he was going to miss him more than Harry would ever know.

—⚏—

43

The sleeping pill Harry gave him did its job to perfection and the plane touched down at JFK ten minutes after it took off from Heathrow. He was still feeling groggy when he stepped outside into a New York blizzard. The warmth of the cab wasn't enough to thaw his fingers so they could grip at the little card with Harry's address on it. The squat Puerto Rican in the driver's seat was staring impatiently at him, as if he was withholding state secrets from him. The driver slipped, skidded and slid his way into the crawling traffic before Cormac's fingers finally remembered their function. He read the address to him Harry had written neatly last night.

D Building
1 W 72nd ST
New York
Zip 10023

The driver let out a whistle and then didn't speak to Cormac for the rest of the journey. Instead, Cormac listened to Puerto Rican music made for sunshine and imagined what the Manhattan skyline looked like outside the window. Somewhere out there in the snow was Bernadette. Somewhere out there might be his future. The comfort of the thought and the remnants of Harry's pill meant he slept the rest of the trip, in spite of the folk festival pulsating from the speaker beside his right ear. When the driver woke him to tell him they'd arrived, he could hardly see the entrance to the building from the car. He pointed to a black lump in the near distance and indicated the entrance was behind it. Cormac carried his bags the short precarious distance to the lump. When he got to it he could make out the Japanese faces of ten or fifteen people who didn't acknowledge him as he skidded past them and into the entrance. He was shaking himself off when the doorman introduced himself in a thick Brooklyn accent.

'You must be Mr O'Reilly. My name's Brendan and it's always a pleasure to meet a fellow Irishman. Harry said you'd be here this morning and I'm under strict instructions to look after you while you're here in New York. The elevator is this way, Sir.'

Cormac followed him across the grand hallway that reminded him more of France than New York. His feet slipped along the floor, which to him, looked like it was carved from the finest oak. The elevator closed behind them. He turned to the immaculately dressed doorman.

'Why is there a group of Japanese people freezing to death outside, Brendan?'

The door opened before he had time to answer. He put the key into the lock and they entered the apartment. Then he spoke.

'You can close your mouth, Sir!'

Cormac couldn't close his mouth. They walked into the grandest apartment he'd ever set foot in. The living room which they now entered was fifty feet in length and the ceilings at least fourteen feet in height. The floor was made of what looked like solid cherry wood. There was a warren of doors branching off the main hallway. He counted at least fifteen. When he came back into the living room, Brendan was lighting the huge log fire that sat against the far wall. Next to it, he flicked a switch which illuminated the majestic silver and gold Christmas tree in the corner of the room. Cormac sat on one of the three huge settees, all of which could comfortably sit five or six people.

Brendan came to the middle of the room and stood about twenty-five feet from him.

'The Japanese tourists are always here, Sir, but more so on this date.'

Cormac was studying the beauty of the ornate windows that dominated the entire right side of the room.

'Why this date?'

'Because it's December 8th, Sir.'

'I don't understand.'

'The day John Lennon was murdered in front of the building.'

Now he understood.

'This is the Dakota Building?'

'It most certainly is, Sir.'

'Harry Crossan has an apartment in the Dakota Building?'

'In my opinion, it's the best apartment in the entire building, Sir, although Harry's only stayed here on three or four occasions since he bought it.'

After he finished shaking his head at how much money could be made from shit, his thoughts turned to Bernadette.

'How far is Broadway from here, Brendan?'

He came and sat three spaces away from him.

'Which theatre are you after, Sir?'

'I don't know.'

'You don't know?'

'Sorry, Brendan, I'm not actually looking for a theatre as such, more a person who works in a theatre. I just don't know which theatre she works in, you see.'

He scratched his chin.

'Well, in that case, Sir, I'd say you're in for a long stay.'

He pointed to the blizzard attacking the windows.

'You may as well be looking for a snowflake in that!'

Cormac felt his enthusiasm drain at the same pace as the colour from his cheeks. How bloody stupid was he to travel all this way to try and find someone in one of the most populated cities in the world, based on one drunken conversation with Harry three months ago? What if she didn't even work on Broadway? What if she had worked on Broadway but now she didn't? What if she'd met somebody and moved away?

What if she'd met somebody?

Oh Jesus! He hadn't even thought of that, had he? She was a beautiful woman whose husband had left her alone and lonely here in a strange city three months ago. Of course she'd met somebody! Of course she had! It was blindingly obvious! Even on the remote chance she hadn't, how the hell was he going to find her? If on the slightest chance he did find her and she was not with someone else, what's to say she'd want to be with him? What had he based that on? One day in Dublin and one fraction of a dance when he'd *imagined* she felt something. He felt an all too familiar stirring.

'Where's the bathroom, Brendan?'

Brendan was where he'd left him when he returned forty minutes later.

'I'm sorry Sir, but I think I may have let my big mouth go before. You obviously need to find this person pretty badly. I know this city like the back of my hand, and if you'll let me, I'd love to help you find her.'

He felt a tiny sensation in his stomach; a momentary flicker that all was not as hopeless as he thought after all.

Brendan was standing and moving towards the door.

'I finish at five. What say we meet over some pizza and a beer and we'll see if we can't put a strategy together that'll help us find the person you're looking for?'

By 11 p.m., Cormac was sitting in the living room with a fuzzy head and a plan. His new friend was fast asleep in one of the bedrooms off the hall. He looked out of the window, which was now clear of snow. He opened it and the sounds of the city tumbled in. Amid the sirens and the car engines, he could make out the sound of a guitar floating up from the front of the building. He lay back in the chair and was content. He was in the same city as her. No matter how long it would take, he would find her. He felt he was finally where he should be. He drifted off to sleep on his first night in New York listening to the sounds of a Japanese John Lennon calling to him from the street below.

'There are places I'll remember
All my life, though some have changed
Some forever not for better
Some are gone and some remain

All these places have their moments
Of lovers and friends I still can recall
Some are dead and some are living
In my life I've loved them all....'

—ɷ—

44

The iPod Annie bought him for Christmas carried him around his hour long jog through Central Park. He smiled to himself at the thought of her sitting in the little flat in Edinburgh selecting and deselecting his 'old man's music' as she called it. She had chosen very well. He'd been jogging every day for the past two months and was forced to buy himself some new jeans before he left England, after his only other pair would no longer stay above his shrinking hips. Today was the best he'd felt in all that time. He was convinced he could run all day. Van Morrison eased his journey around the tree-lined path. He enjoyed watching his breath blow freezing fog around his face. Through it, he could still marvel at Manhattan rising proudly into the clear blue sky draped all around it. All that remained of the snow were the dozen or more decomposing corpses of yesterday's snowmen lying lifeless and melting by the side of the lake. He left Van and Madame George 'down on Cyprus Avenue' as he reached the entrance to the building, which he could now appreciate for the first time in all its Gothic splendour. The Japanese pilgrims were no longer at the front door, but had decamped to the tranquillity of Strawberry Fields behind him. He could hear a faint guitar emanating from beneath a swaying elm. He saw Brendan scouring the newspaper at his desk as he entered the building. By the time their conversation finished last night, fuelled by too many beers but thankfully only one slice of pizza on Cormac's part, they convinced each other finding Bernadette was not going to be too difficult at all. In fact, if anything, it was going to be pretty straightforward. There were only thirty-nine theatres currently in operation on Broadway. If he was efficient, with Brendan's help and contacts, he could probably have them all covered in a day. It was that thought more than Van that whisked him through Central Park as New York was still waking, if it actually managed to get any sleep in the first place. He was still buoyed by the prospect when he approached Brendan, who didn't look up until Cormac was standing over the paper and blocking the light from the door.

'Good morning, Cormac. I'm sorry about crashing at your place last night. It was very unprofessional of me. I promise I won't do that again. Please don't tell the management company, otherwise, I'll be fired.'

Cormac put his hand on the pristine green sleeve of his frock coat.

'Relax, Brendan. To tell you the truth, I was glad of the company. I've never been one for staying anywhere on my own. As far as I'm concerned, you can stay any night you like while I'm here. Anyway, we've more important business to sort out than sleeping arrangements.'

Brendan's expression indicated he took little comfort in Cormac's reassuring response. Either that or something else was troubling him.

'What's up with your face, Brendan?'

He lifted his hand from the paper and pushed it across to Cormac. He showed him the list of Broadway theatres. He then ran his finger along the considerably longer list of 'Off Broadway' theatres. By the time he finished explaining that these lists didn't include what was by far the longest list of all, the 'Off Off Broadway' theatres, which were not actually even on Broadway itself, but scattered all over this vast city of eight million people, Cormac was forced to take a seat next to him behind the desk. They sat in silence and stared at the page. Four long columns of theatres and shows occupied four-fifths of the page. Squeezed in along the right side was a single column where some critic was savaging the latest show to open at The Beacon. Cormac idly read the column to take his mind of the impossible task he'd set himself. He was glad he wasn't part of the show being critiqued. Brendan stared blankly at the elevator as he spoke.

'Cormac, she could be anywhere in the city. I'm not saying she'll be impossible to find. I'm just saying it could take you weeks, months even, to find her. If she's here at all, that is.'

Cormac finished reading the column. He felt the familiar activity in the pit of his stomach.

'She could be anywhere in the city, I'll grant you, but she's not!'

'I don't understand Cormac?'

He pushed the newspaper over to him.

'Look at the column on the right.'

'What am I looking at?'

'The writer's name there on the bottom corner.'

'B.J. Fitzgerald?'

'Her middle name is Jane and her married name is Fitzgerald. It's her, I can feel it! She's not anywhere, Brendan. She's right here in front of me!'

Brendan clearly did not share his enthusiasm.

'Do you have any idea how many Irish there are in New York? There are millions! Do you know how many of them are called Fitzgerald? I'd guess thousands!'

Cormac was not daunted at the thought at all. Instead he was back on his feet and scribbling down the address for Bernadette Jane Fitzgerald onto the pad next to Brendan's unconvinced and still shaking head.

'Where is Amsterdam Avenue?'

'Just off Broadway.'

'How far is that from here?'

Brendan took the pad from him. He pulled out a map.

'Let's see, 334 Amsterdam Avenue. I'd say twenty-five, thirty minutes from here. I'll mark it on the map for you.'

Cormac snatched it and began to jog to the door.

'Hey, wait up! If it is her, and I'm telling you there's more chance it's some hairy fat grease-ball who sits on his ass at a computer all day in between snacking, I think you should at least tidy yourself up a bit, don't you?'

After a quick change and a reluctant breakfast with Brendan, he turned down 72nd Street and followed the map towards Broadway. He tried to control his racing heartbeat for the first ten minutes until he gave up and joined it. He jogged the rest of the way in his jeans and boots. His hair was wet with sweat and his feet were hot with blisters when he arrived at the tall building on Amsterdam Avenue just after midday. The front door was locked and the whole length of the wall next to it was filled with buzzers and corresponding addresses. He scanned them all twice and there was definitely no address for a B.J. Fitzgerald. He studied them again, slower this time. The fifth one from the top looked familiar; it read: *New York Writer's Workshop*. He was certain that's what was written below the name on the article. He took a deep breath and pushed the button. Nothing happened for a second, and then the wall spoke to him in a tinny voice.

'New York Writer's Workshop, how may I help?'

He shouted into the silver box.

'I'm looking for B. J. Fitzgerald?'

'Do you have an appointment, Sir?'

'No, I'm a friend.'

'Sir, if you are a friend, you'll know you cannot gain access to the building without an appointment!'

'Yes, I'm sorry, of course. Could you just tell me if B. J. Fitzgerald is Irish … and a girl?'

'Sir, forgive me, but I'm not authorised to provide such information and even if I were, I sure wouldn't be providing it to a 'friend' who doesn't even know if B.J. is a man or a woman! Good day!'

He buzzed twice more before crossing the street and preparing himself for a long wait.

There was no activity in the next tortuous four hours. So little activity, in fact, he was convinced the voice in the wall was the only employee in the entire building. He'd counted at least forty separate buzzers alongside the huge red door and yet no one had entered, or left, since he'd arrived at midday. His back ached from standing, and his blisters were rubbing on the heels of his boots. At 5:30 the door opened and a pale, fat, white middle-aged man waddled out, in front of a fatter and younger black woman. They chatted for a short while, before B. J. and the voice in the wall parted with a cheery wave to each other. He waited another thirty minutes in the freezing darkness just in case, before finally deciding he'd get a cab back to the Dakota. It was only the first day he'd been actively looking for her. He was disappointed, but not disheartened.

He didn't see the door opening, but saw the three figures emerge from the darkness opposite. Two young thirty-something men exited the building together and partially obscured the smaller figure behind. They started walking to their right, towards Broadway. He crossed the street with the intention of falling in behind them to see if he could get a better look. By halfway across the street, he established that the third figure was female. His heart quickened. By the time he reached the curb he could see the beret on her head and he could hear the thump in his chest. One look at her gait and he knew it was her. As she walked, she trailed her right foot across the ground. It was a habit he'd noticed when she was just fifteen, shortly after they met, and it was obviously one she was not willing to give up on. He felt his heart trying to escape its mooring. He opened his mouth to call to her, but her left arm wouldn't let him. As they turned onto Broadway, the neon lights followed her arm's path until it merged with the right arm of the man strolling next to her. He followed her beret in the crowd as it turned off Broadway until five minutes later it disappeared through a tiny door on the left off Columbus Avenue.

For the second time that day, he stood across the street from a building she sat in. He watched the inviting warm glow radiating from the window of the little pub while attempting to blow some life into his numb and tingling fingers. Thirty minutes later, she left with one of the men. He felt his stomach churn and was grateful that he was close to a pub with a toilet. He watched them turn left just next to the pub. He crossed the street and turned the corner. He needed to speak to her. The alleyway was dark and completely deserted!

—⋙—

45

Only after he surfaced from the bathroom situated adjacent to the front door was he able to take a proper look around the little pub. It had a long bar to the right and four booths to the left. The small group, of nine or ten mainly male clientele, were all smartly dressed and probably a regular after-work crowd. It was a tired little place that had seen better days, and its walls consisted of nothing but several faded Guinness posters. He could make out Journey singing 'Don't Stop Believing' over the chatter of the regulars and was still deciding what his next course of action would be when the barman shouted to him in a Belfast accent.

'Will you be staying for a drink, Mr O'Reilly, or are you just in to use our facilities?'

He was still attempting to programme the fact that he knew his name, when the pale, ponytailed barman came around the bar to greet him.

'I'm sorry; it is Cormac O'Reilly MP, isn't it? Or should I say former MP? It's just your face was plastered all over the papers and the TV back home in the summer. Mind, you do look a bit thinner up close.'

Journey stopped and The Rolling Stones started. That, and the warm handshake from the long-haired barman, with '100% Irish' splashed across his green T-shirt, convinced him staying for one drink wouldn't do any harm.

The beer was cold and sharp and the music got better and louder. The crowd dwindled to just two or three hardy souls in the booth nearest the door. Cormac sat at the end of the bar, furthest from the door, whilst Mick stood directly opposite, firing question after question at him about last summer's events. When he had completely exhausted his repertoire and fell silent for a brief interlude, Cormac decided it was his turn.

'The three people who were here earlier, two men and a woman, they came in about 6:15, do you see them much in here?'

He didn't pause to consider.

'Oh, you mean Danny, Paul, and Bernadette?'

Cormac nodded for him to continue.

'They come in every night at the same time and then Danny and Bernadette leave after one drink. Paul stays for another and his wife picks him up about ten minutes later. They're all writers and Bernie is a bit of a singer by all accounts. They're a nice crew.'

Cormac shifted in his seat and asked a question he didn't want to know the answer to.

'Are Danny and Bernadette a couple, then?'

'I'd say they are, sort of.'

Cormac felt a gentle pounding in his head, but persevered.

'What do you mean, sort of?'

'Well, they live together somewhere around here.'

Cormac put his hand to his face to hold his sagging mouth in position. He knew he shouldn't have asked, yet he needed to know.

'They share an apartment because they couldn't afford to rent on their own this close to work.'

'So they're not a couple, then?'

Mick laughed.

'Not as far as I'm aware. Danny has a boyfriend upstate he spends weekends with and Bernie is divorced or in the process of it anyway.'

Cormac had already leaned across the bar and kissed him on the forehead before he had finished the sentence.

'Are you in the mood to help an old man with a twenty-two year problem?'

He raised his hand and Cormac felt obliged to slap it, but not before checking to see if anyone was watching.

'I'm only too happy to help a fellow Irishmen in distress. What did you have in mind?'

Cormac pointed to the wall of CDs behind his head.

'Can I have a look at your record collection?'

—ᴍ—

46

He stood outside and checked his watch. He had one minute to wait. He'd spent an agonisingly sleepless night and a restless day at Harry's place. He'd thought about taking in the sights of the city but couldn't bring himself to do anything except pace up and down the living room. Instead, he'd walked back and forth and studied his watch, which on several occasions he'd brought impatiently to his ear to make sure it was still working. He looked at the watch again. It was time!

He opened the door with an unsteady hand and stepped inside on unreliable legs. He nodded to his accomplice and listened to the first bars of the song. She was sitting on a stool and had her back to him. He saw her glance up in a flicker of recognition before she continued with her conversation. He walked slowly behind her, now on steadier legs and reached her halfway through the intro. His accomplice in the green T-shirt spoke to her.

'Excuse me, Bernadette - my friend would like to ask you something.'

She spun on her stool.

He looked into her eyes and forced the words out through his desert of a mouth.

'Bernadette, would you do me the honour of dancing with me?'

She hesitated for a moment, before she slipped off the stool and placed her arms gently on his shoulders as the singer found his voice.

'A Love struck Romeo, sings a streetsuss serenade
Laying everybody low, with a love song that he made
Finds a convenient street light, step's out of the shade
And says something like, you and me babe how
about it?'

She moved closer. He felt his heart beating faster and louder than it ever had before. Until he realised it was hers. They swayed in silence as the song gently faded and died. He let go of her so he could look at her.

But she was gone!

He saw the door closing behind her. This time he didn't wait. He was at the door and into the street before it closed. She was running now towards Broadway. He ran after her. He called her name. She didn't stop. She ran into the glare of the neon lights. He felt the burning of yesterday's blisters but didn't stop. He couldn't stop. He felt the fear in his stomach but didn't stop. He knew if he lost sight of her, he'd never see her again. For the moment, he could see her clearly. She was just in front of him. He called after her again.

'Bernadette, please stop! Please don't leave me here! I beg you, please stay with me! Don't leave me here on my own!'

She turned right. He turned to follow her and ran straight into the chest of a startled and now tumbling theatre-goer. He picked himself and the uninjured, but swearing tourist off the freezing pavement. His eyes searched the illuminated street. He started to run, but he didn't know the direction she had gone. He slowed and stopped at the end of the street. There were three roads branching off in different directions. He ran to the edge of each of them. It was hopeless. She was gone! He fell to his knees. He tore at his shirt. He screamed her name. But he knew. It was finally over.

He was still sobbing and mumbling incoherently when he was aware of someone standing in front of him. He wiped his face with the back of his jacket.

'I'm sorry - I'll be out of here in a second.'

He picked himself off the floor. He could feel the contents of his nose running down his throat and his face. It hurt to open his swollen eyes. He focused on the figure in front of him and through the haze of his tears he could make out the black tram lines on her pale cheeks.

'Bernadette?'

He could see her face now flashing in the light. It was full of steely determination.

'I came back Cormac to finish this properly once and for all.'

He felt his eyes betray him and knew his stomach would follow.

'Too much time has passed, Cormac. I don't think I can go back there. I don't think my heart can take the pain when you leave me again. You see, I would have given my life to you. I did give my life to you for a long time, even after you had gone. I don't think I can take the pain. So I came back to ask you not to bother me anymore. Goodbye, Cormac.'

He looked down at her outstretched hand and watched his own as it touched hers. She began to walk away from him. He felt his chest pounding and his legs buckle.

'Wait, Bernadette! Wait with me just for a little while.'

She turned to look at him and waited for him to speak. He tried to say something, but his mouth couldn't find the words. She started to walk away again. Then he let his heart talk to her instead.

'I've been running away all my life. I've been desperately searching for happiness. I've been trying to find somewhere I can call my home. When I think of the last time I wasn't running, that I was truly happy, that I was home, it was when I was in my bedroom in Killane. You were lying beside me. It was your 18th birthday.'

His eyes began to sting again. She stopped walking. He continued talking.

'We weren't speaking, we were just lying there. There was music playing. I didn't know it at the time but I do now - I was the luckiest man in the world that day, Bernadette, because I had your love. I know I lost it. I know I hurt you too much, but I hurt myself more. Through my own stupidity, I lost your love. I've been trying to replace it for twenty-two years. I know now I cannot. I just want you to know before you go I will be sorry for the rest of my life. I want you to know whatever happens in your life, even if we never meet again, I have always loved you, even when I left you behind, and I always will love you, even when you leave me behind tonight.'

The contents of his nose were now pouring down his face, and he could no longer see her. He didn't see her wipe her face and take her first step towards him. He only knew she was there when he felt her gentle hand brush his cheek. She spoke through her tears and into his chest.

'You never lost my love, Cormac, and no matter how many times I try to tell myself otherwise, you never will lose it. I remember your room. I remember how I felt that day. I was just a girl, but I knew my heart. I knew then what I was feeling was special. I was certain then I would never love anyone the way I loved you that day before you left. I was so sure it would last a lifetime. In spite of myself, I can't help myself but I still feel the same way. It just won't go away.'

He took her hand in his.

'When do you have to go home again, Cormac?'

He didn't answer. She asked again.

'When do you have to go home again?'

He lifted her head and pulled her to him.

'I'm already home, Bernadette. I'm already home.'

He held on and knew he would never let go again.

They swayed together under the flashing neon sign. They were just another Irish boy and Irish girl holding on to each other somewhere in New York City.

It's an age old story....

THE END

Lightning Source UK Ltd.
Milton Keynes UK
UKOW051925040112

184747UK00001B/8/P